FLESH and BLOOD

To Dawn, George and Isobel – my world

STRIPES PUBLISHING
An imprint of Little Tiger Press
1 The Coda Centre, 189 Munster Road,
London SW6 6AW

This paperback edition first published in Great Britain in 2015

ISBN: 978-1-84715-456-9

Printed and bound in the UK.

10 9 8 7 6 5 4 3 2 1

FLESH and BLOOD

SIMON CHESHIRE

Chapter One

I didn't want things to turn out this way. I really didn't.

There have been deaths, and worse. Even if there's no blood on my hands, not directly, I have to face the consequences of my actions, of what I *did* do. If events had happened differently, if I hadn't been so intent on following my theories, then perhaps I wouldn't be here now, sitting at this desk, writing out what some might see as a confession. But, if I hadn't reacted as I did, then I'd never have found out everything I uncovered. I had to try, didn't I?

Maybe I could have prevented some of it. Maybe I could have saved a life or two, if only I'd acted sooner. No, that's not true. I acted soon enough. I think.

Nobody believed me, except Liam and Jo. And they didn't take me seriously, at first.

When did I last sleep? I don't remember. It doesn't matter, I guess.

I have to write. I have to tell myself to stop being a pathetic baby and be calm and rational. That's what I have to do. I must record the facts, a sequence of events, the chain of suspicions and thoughts that have led me to where I am now. So that, when someone reads this, they understand.

At least it's quiet right now, and I can collect my thoughts. This desk I'm sitting at is small and antique. A really nice piece of furniture. You can see the dark grain of the wood, the years displayed in its warm colour, its soft shine. The notebook has smooth, off-white paper. It almost seems a shame to write in it, but of course I must. I have to set down everything, to document it, from the beginning.

I have to think clearly. Breathe deeply.

I'll sit and think for a while. Then I'll write.

I must begin on 18th September. That was the day we moved into No. 3, Priory Mews. A matter of weeks ago.

My name is Sam Hunter. That's Sam as in Samuel, but I hate being called Samuel. Only my gran calls me Samuel. That's my mum's mum. She still talks to me as if I'm five, even though I'm seventeen.

I'm OK at school work. I normally hover around a B-grade. I keep my room tidy, when I can be bothered to, or when friends are coming round. I like films, graphic novels, regularly changing the posters on my walls, and those chocolate bars you can get with marzipan inside. I'm not keen on sport, and I don't like vegetables. Maybe I'm still five after all.

I have parents, unfortunately.

My mum is one of those mothers who spends every minute she possibly can at work and the rest of the time moaning about how much time she spends working. She's employed by a bank, and has been since she left school at my age. Twenty-five years, slowly climbing the corporate ladder. A very slow climb. Up just three rungs, Assistant Cashier to Deputy Thingummy of Accounting, whatever it is she's called now. You have to admire her determination, I guess. Also her ability to work around money all day long and never once nicking any of it. I don't think I'd be able to keep up the same level of will power. Even so, it's had its effect. She assesses everything and everyone according to the amount of cash involved. Except my dad, that is.

Dad's a musician. It's not as interesting as it sounds. Mostly, he sits around the house and strums at his guitar, or phones his friends 'in the business' and goes to the pub. Middle-age spread has been piling on the pounds for a while now, and he's kept the same scraggy ponytail since about 1995. I try to keep him away from school functions.

In his late teens, he joined a punk band called The Howling Sirens. The punk movement had just ended. They had one very minor hit, then split up. Dad's been reliving the glory days ever since, spending money we didn't have on the latest recording gear, or on worthless tat he claims is rock 'n' roll memorabilia. He's a dreamer. Not that being a dreamer is a bad thing in itself, but he's lazy with it. His idea of a full day is lying on the sofa and staring out of the window.

Don't get me wrong, I do love my parents, on the whole. They've always been as good to me as circumstances allow, but they're not the easiest of people to cheer for, if you see what I mean.

As a family, we'd always been just-scrape-by, go-without-to-pay-the-bills people, until recently. We're something approaching minted now. I'll get to why in a minute. It's the reason we ended up in Priory Mews. For as long as I can remember, we've lived at a series of run-down addresses in a series of run-down streets. Until Priory Mews.

For several years, we lived in a flat above a newsagent's. I really liked that place, because I could get comics and magazines for free. The guy who ran the shop would let me rummage through the stuff he was going to return to the wholesaler.

I read a lot of American Marvel and DC comics. I read film review journals and blokey stuff about computers, which made me feel grown-up. I'd gaze over the cultural sections of the Sunday papers, getting glimpses of a wider world that seemed sophisticated and stylish.

The newsagent had a rack of paperbacks, too, and I'd got through all the James Bonds and several Stephen Kings before I was twelve. It was exciting, almost magical, finding something new. The thrill of discovery.

Looking back now, I think the newsagent allowed me all those freebies because he felt sorry for me. At the time, the look on his face seemed like kindly indulgence, but now I'm older I can see he was wondering if I was OK, what with Mum at work all hours and Dad off somewhere or asleep.

But I was fine. I relished the freedom. I could watch telly in peace. They lived in their own little worlds, and so did I. All that solitary rummaging through the newsagent's boxes did me a big favour: without it, I might never have become interested in journalism. That was the fully formed idea that popped into my head when the word 'career' was first mentioned at school. It was swiftly followed by a resolution not to approach adulthood like my parents. I was going to make more of myself, I was going to do better.

We lived in two or three Midlands towns, moving according to which bank branch Mum was assigned to, but the upgrade to Priory Mews took us eighty miles closer to London. Closer to Dad's cronies and the music biz, because it was his 'career' that called the shots now.

Hadlington is a picture postcard of English suburbia. I'd never even heard of it before I was told we were going to live there. In the early afternoon of Wednesday 18th September, I watched it roll past me from the back seat of the (brand-new) car.

Clipped lawns, detached properties, lines of shops all still in business instead of boarded up. Mothers wheeling pushchairs with a smile, old folk chatting at bus stops as the bus pulled in on time, corner cafés filled with suited customers tapping at their iPads.

"Shall we drive around a bit before we go to the house?" said Mum, slowing the car at traffic lights. "Go for a wander about town?"

"Let's do that, babe," said Dad, his voice thick with excitement. "Take a look at the manor."

They took my silence for agreement. We drove past an industrial park plastered with freshly printed hoardings: engineering works, small caterers, e-tail warehouses, an art studio. I remember lounging on the back seat, the car's smoothly efficient shock absorbers still feeling like a novelty, and looking in vain for anything that reminded me of our Old Life.

Everything here was tidy, and clean, and nice-looking. Even the factory units were smartly designed. Nothing was dumped on front drives in Hadlington. Here they had civic pride. Here they had money, and responsible attitudes, and a spring in their step. It shone out of the streets, the buildings, the pavements. This is Hadlington, said the town, and it's *better* than where you come from.

We drove around the southern half of the town, skirting the grounds of the large Elizabethan mansion that was the local tourist attraction, with New Car smell filling my lungs and the engine purring like a tamed big cat. Here were leafy avenues and clusters of homes surrounding oval-shaped greens with little children playing while parents watched from wooden benches. We crossed the humped, stone bridge that spans the river close to that Elizabethan mansion.

The River Arvan slices through Hadlington like a knife through flesh, its sinuous waters slow and dark. It cuts through a picturesque park, where trees and the occasional fishing platform dot its banks. Then it leads out of town, getting deeper and more treacherous as it goes, with swirling undercurrents and tangled weeds. People drown in it regularly, I later discovered.

As the river leads out of town, it borders the Elton Gardens estate, Hadlington's own enclave of the underclass. Most towns and cities have their run-down areas, but Elton Gardens stands in such contrast to the rest of the town that it almost seems like a broad blade of the outside world trying to stab its way in.

The rest of Hadlington looks down on the residents of Elton Gardens in a way I'll always find repellent. Snobbish, dismissive, wilfully ill-informed. The residents of Elton Gardens either work in the town's least desirable jobs, or scratch an existence on the edges of the law. Kids from Elton Gardens go to the schools along the A-road that heads towards London, the sort of schools you see in Channel 4 documentaries designed to shock the middle classes.

The estate was apparently quite smart when it was built in the late 1960s but it rapidly declined. The final nail in its coffin were the floods of 2007 and 2012, when the Arvan burst its banks and gurgled up from the drains, gushing across the ground floors of all two hundred and twenty-seven homes. There was sodden rubbish in the streets for months.

On hot days in the summer, so I learned, teenagers jump off the clattering green metal footbridge that crosses the river beside the estate. They don't listen to the warnings, of course. Two or three times a year, there's a huge headline in the local paper, above a picture of the grieving family. Sometimes, people get pulled under and the bodies are never found.

At least, so it's believed.

We didn't drive around the estate. We'd just left that kind of place.

The park and the estate border one side of the river while, up a steep and landscaped hill, Maybrick Road runs parallel with it on the other. Maybrick Road is the poshest part of Hadlington. That's where you find Maybrick High School and five-bed detached houses that cost six times the national average. People put themselves into serious debt just to send their kids to Maybrick High and have a Maybrick Road address.

Priory Mews joins Maybrick Road a few hundred metres from the school. Gently swaying trees, pleasant views down the hill towards the park and river. Bins and recycling boxes out of sight. When we drove into the short cul-de-sac on that Wednesday afternoon, the removal van was already parked outside our new home. The car glided to a halt and we got out, my door clunking behind me with a deliciously expensive *wh-ump*.

Mum bustled over to the three removal men, who were propped up against the side of the van smoking.

She fumbled in her bag for the house keys.

Dad leaned against the front of the car and gazed around, a grin lighting up his chubby features. "You made it, sunshine," he said to himself quietly.

To be honest, I could see his point. I was grinning, too. There were three detached houses nestled in a semicircle: big, solid homes with curving bay windows and smoothly tarmacked drives. Ours was the one on the left, No. 3.

This was the first time I'd ever seen it, except for in the estate agent's photos. Mum and Dad had only visited it once before paying the full asking price.

Dad had made a million. Or near enough. Out of the blue, two songs he'd written in the 90s got picked up by a trendy girl band and became global hits. 'Sweet Angel' and 'Boppin' Hoppin'', by the Blaster Rays – you must have heard them. Dad wrote them as solid guitar rock, and they got turned into cheesy pop. Utterly hideous; I actually felt sorry for my father. But worldwide sales, downloads, radio airplay, stadium performances – they all added up to a lot of money. Suddenly, we were quite rich. Mum grabbed her chance and we got a Maybrick Road address. No. 3, Priory Mews, Maybrick Road, Hadlington.

While the removal men were unloading our stuff, ninety per cent of which was Dad's assorted 'treasures', Mum and Dad skipped about the empty house like a couple of kids. You could hear Dad's whooping echo off the walls.

The house was great. Two enormous living rooms downstairs, a couple of little rooms at the back, a kitchen with a long annexe leading out into the garden. Upstairs, five bedrooms, the ugliest bathroom I'd ever seen, and a narrow door opening on to creaky wooden stairs up to a vast and dusty attic space.

My room was at the front corner of the house. Or rather, rooms. There was an en-suite shower room at one end, and at the other was what I presume was meant as a walk-in wardrobe, lined with shelving painted in off-white gloss and with three chrome hanging rails. It alone was larger than most of the rooms I'd ever called my own.

We lived here now. Not in some just-for-now, until-we-can-afford-something-else, stop-gap place, but *here*. Everything I owned filled two big cardboard boxes beside the door.

It was only when I stood beside my wide window,

overlooking the removal van and the front of the house, that I noticed the fourth building in Priory Mews. How I'd missed it outside, I'll never know. Too busy gaping at our place, I suppose.

From the moment I saw it, it unsettled me.

It was set well back from the others, surrounded by tall, narrow shrubs like leafy security guards. A broad gravel pathway led up to an imposing entrance. The house was three storeys high, its two lower levels topped with a series of windows jutting out from very high, angular sections of roof. One of these sections rose up even taller than the others, punctuated by chimney breasts. At the corners, the walls had the kind of inlaid stone you see on old manor houses and castles, like zigzag reinforcements.

The house was more than double the size of the others in Priory Mews. A long, glassy ground-floor extension had been added at the side. Above loomed the tortured, twisted grey branches of ancient wych elms and silver birches in the back garden. A separate, modern two-door garage had been built closer to the road.

This, I later found out, was Bierce Priory, built in 1812. That extension was constructed in the 1920s, at the same time as our house. Even at first sight, even with the excitement of the moment sending my mood soaring, the Priory looked cold and austere. As if it was watching me back.

Despite my impressions of the place, I paid no more attention to the Priory that day. Now, merely writing the name sends a rush of horror through my guts. We had Chinese takeaway for tea, and Mum and I spent hours dragging cardboard boxes from one room to another. Dad spotted our new neighbours at No. 2 getting into their car, an elderly couple, and called them over with a whistle and a wave. I didn't catch their names but they seemed taken in by that studied chumminess of his. He talked at them for nearly twenty minutes, while they smiled blandly.

I hooked up the TV in the biggest living room. The sound bounced off the bare floorboards as I sat on our threadbare sofa. I patted its stained arm a couple of times. *You'll be chucked out soon, old friend*, I thought to myself, *without a doubt*. I watched gangsters shoot each other while Mum scrubbed the bathroom and Dad clattered about. "Ellen! Where did you pack my... S'OK, babe, I found them!"

By eleven I was snuggled down on my mattress on the floor of my room. The pieces of my wooden bed frame were stacked in a corner, waiting for when I could be bothered to put them together. My anglepoise lamp threw a yellowy glow over the thick paperback anthology of '70s *Doctor Strange* comics I'd got on eBay just before we moved.

I was starting at Maybrick High the following day, Thursday. I'd tried to squeeze a couple of days off, to start at the beginning of a week, but with the school only a two-minute walk away and me already being late for the start of the Maybrick term, I had no excuses. I yawned, clicked off the light and went to sleep.

When I got up, Mum had already left for work. Some things never change. She didn't need to do that job any more, but she did it anyway. I had suggested to her that she could free up her job for someone who really needed the money, but she'd just looked at me as if I'd asked her to boil her head. The only difference now was that she'd chosen which bank branch to work in, rather than letting the bank send her anywhere it liked. I imagined that the Hadlington branch was a little more prestigious than the last one.

I was up, washed and dressed nearly an hour before I needed to leave. I got through two slices of toast and a mug of orange juice, with first-day nerves jangling at my stomach. I made my sandwiches with a care I never normally took. Displacement activity, to mask the jitters. Cake in my lunchbox? Did I want cake today?

I still had forty minutes before I needed to leave. I took a slow tour of the house. The silence was only broken by the clump of my shoes on the floorboards and the sound of Dad snoring.

I told myself not to be such a wuss. No need to be nervous. Best school in the district.

I checked myself in the unhung mirror in the hall. My new uniform was embarrassingly fresh and unworn. My stomach knotted all over again.

Outside, the air was sharp and damp, a fresh autumnal morning. I looked across to our two neighbouring houses, but nothing was stirring there. Opposite them, the Priory seemed a touch less sinister in the cold early light, glowering behind its spiky shrubs.

As soon as I walked out on to Maybrick Road, I could tell something was up. There was a steady flow of uniformed kids along the pavements. From the end of Priory Mews, you could just see the main entrance to the school, but kids were going straight past it. They were hurriedly crossing the road and taking a wide path that led down the hill, ending at the green metal footbridge over the river, which led to the park and the corner of Elton Gardens.

As a handful of younger pupils passed me, I stopped one of them.

"What's going on?" I asked.

"Dead body!" said the kid excitedly. "A Year Nine's put a picture on Facebook." He and his friends scurried on.

A what? Surely he meant an animal or something? A larger group of pupils, who looked my age, also crossed the road and headed for the path. I wondered if some of them were my new classmates. I allowed curiosity to drag me into the flow.

The path sloped in long, graceful curves down to the river. To either side were broad stretches of grass, and beyond that sprouted bushy swathes of tall reeds and sedges.

As the flow of kids approached the river, I could

see a gathering arranged in a ragged semicircle. I'd almost caught up with the group who looked my age, but hung back. I wasn't sure if the best way to meet classmates was rubbernecking at the scene of an … accident?

A girl suddenly detached herself from the semicircle, staggered a few metres and vomited noisily on to the grass. A couple of her friends rushed to her side.

By now I was at the spot where the gathering of pupils had trampled flat a haphazard patch of the reeds. I could see something stretched out on the ground. Someone was saying that a woman walking her dog had found it a few minutes ago, that she'd already called the police. For a second, the scene flashed through my head: the dog sniffing around, not coming when called, taking a few licks.

I drew closer. I saw it in detail now.

My first day nerves vanished, replaced by icy horror.

It was a man, flat on his back on the damp ground, legs pointing away from me. He was dressed in dirty trainers, fleece tracksuit bottoms and a jumper. His limbs were straight, as if he'd calmly lain down on the spot. His face was upturned; dull staring eyes pointed at the grey sky.

His face was spotted with blood. Much more blood, long sprays of it, fanned out around his head like some hideous spiked wig. The top of his head was gone. He simply ended, just above the face, sliced open like a pepper.

Chapter Two

"Someone's taken his brain!" cried the kid I'd stopped up on Maybrick Road.

"Eurgh, I bet that woman's dog had it!" squirmed one of his friends.

The others groaned in disgust.

There was an empty, blood-smeared bowl of skull where the man's brain had once been. I stepped back, almost without thinking. It was difficult to take in what I was seeing.

Suddenly, there was a general rush of pupils away up the path. At the same moment, I heard a single whoop from a police siren. A patrol car had driven across the park's lawns, leaving muddy indentations, and was parked beside the footbridge. Two officers, a man and a woman, were dashing across the river.

"Get away from there, you kids! Don't touch anything! Has anyone touched anything?"

There was a chorus of "no"s and "no way"s.

Pupils scattered and scurried back towards the school, looking over their shoulders as they went.

A woman I hadn't spotted until now, with a white West Highland terrier bouncing around her, intercepted the female police officer and they started talking in hushed tones. The male officer jogged over to the corpse, let out a short exclamation at the sight of it and immediately radioed for backup.

I was more than a dozen metres away by now. Everyone was running, as if a gruesome creature was snapping at our heels. The younger ones laughed and shouted, while the older ones merely threw wide-eyed looks at each other.

I don't really remember what happened for a few minutes after that. My mind went a bit numb. I must have gone to the school reception, to tell them I'd arrived. I presumably waited, then the Deputy Head must have collected me and led me to his office.

It was a pokey little room on the top floor of the main building, with a narrow floor-to-ceiling window, looking out on to the sports field. His desk was a litter of papers and dog-eared paperbacks. I sat below a cluttered corkboard. The Deputy Head himself, Mr Stainsby, was one of those naturally scruffy people who can't look smart to save their lives.

Only now, for some reason, did the obvious thought flash into my mind: that was a murder, in the park. A killing.

"Well, it's great to welcome you to our school, Steve," he began, pulling out drawers and looking for something.

"Sam," I said.

"Sorry, yes, Sam." He searched among his papers. "OKaaay, I'm afraid I'm filling in for the Head; he normally likes to have a chat with new students, but he's away at a leadership seminar. I hope you're feeling up to today's challenges. Forgive me, but I just heard a moment ago there was some sort of incident in the park? You didn't happen to see anything, did you?"

The man had been horribly murdered. Cut open.

"Er, no, I didn't see anything," I said, not wanting to talk about it.

"Oh, right, OK," he said, finally pulling out a slim file. "The Office was, umm... Anyway, here's your timetable; we're on the two-week system here – are you familiar with that?"

"Yes, we had the same thing at my last school," I said, taking the sheet of paper from him.

He consulted the file. "I've got the reports here from your last school. You're clearly an excellent student, which is great, but it does look as if you'll have some catching up to do. In most of your subjects, we're further along in the curriculum than you were at –" he flicked a sheet – "Oak Vale."

"What will I need to do?"

"Best action plan is to talk with your form tutor, who is… Miss Marlo. I was going to say that I'll give you a whistlestop tour of the school first, but I think…" He checked his watch. "I think if I take you down to your form room right now, I can hand you over to Miss Marlo straight away. How's that sound?" He looked up at me and grinned.

"Fine," I smiled. Already I didn't like him.

He led me back through a labyrinth of corridors and stairwells, much of it laced with the mixed odours of air freshener and human beings. My nerves began to jangle again. I got looked at quizzically by everyone we passed. New face.

Miss Marlo taught English, and her classroom was at the end of a wide walkway covered in pictures of writers and some poster-sized reproductions of famous book covers. Mr Stainsby knocked once and marched inside. I followed him meekly, conscious that everyone in the room would be examining me, marking me out of ten for coolness and acceptability. I wondered if I should try to act casual. Or would that look obvious?

My new form tutor was younger than my parents, very blonde and very thin. As Mr Stainsby came into the room, she swung round. Her expression was flustered.

"Mr Stainsby, I need a word at once," she said in a low voice. Looking at her, and at the thirty other faces in the room, I guessed she'd just been told about the corpse.

The two teachers bustled out into the corridor, Miss Marlo pointedly shutting the door behind her. I was left standing there, up in front of the whiteboard. The whole class did exactly what I'd expected them to do: stare right at me. There was a pause.

"Awkward!" I said loudly.

They all laughed, a release of tension via a weak joke. As if on cue, the bell rang. Everyone rose, chair legs scraping loudly.

I recognized a couple of faces from the group that I'd shadowed down the path to the river. One of them was blinking back tears, and I assumed it was them who'd told Miss Marlo what had happened.

Everyone was shouldering bags, shuffling out and chattering to each other. Miss Marlo suddenly appeared at my side. "Hello, sorry about that. Do you have your timetable?"

"Yes, I do."

"Come back here at break; we can talk then. For now, we'll just have to throw you in at the deep end." She fluttered a hand at a tall boy who was shuffling out with the others. "Liam, you're a sensible lad – can you take Steve Hunter here under your wing this morning?"

"Sure," said Liam. He had small eyes and a slightly chunky nose, topped with a dense mop of brown hair. He clearly wasn't too keen on having the new kid tag along. "What's your first lesson?"

I whipped a look at my timetable. "Er, history."

"Most of us, too; follow me. H3."

We were halfway down the corridor outside, squashed in the mass of students, me trying not to lose sight of the back of Liam's head, when he turned and spoke again. "Steve, is it?"

"Sam," I said.

"Sam, OK," he said.

History was fine, mostly. Maths likewise. I was gawped at, and issued textbooks, and singled out by teachers, and called Steve. It had to be wrong on a vital piece of paper somewhere.

The contrast between the pupils of Maybrick High and those of my last school was so huge as to be almost comical. Oak Vale was a school where there was a daily fight beside the bike shelters, where a twitchy weirdo in an anorak sold drugs to sixth formers outside the gate, and the Head banged on about league tables being unimportant in the broader picture. It was the sort of place where teachers kept saying how every kid was 'brilliant' and every piece of work 'incredible' in order to cover up how dismal and bad it all was, until whatever they said became meaningless. I didn't really have any friends there, not proper friends, and I'd been glad to leave it all behind.

Maybrick High kids were far more affluent, that's for sure. Many had the self-assured confidence you see in people who come from a history of money: the unspoken assumptions, the certainty of approval and advantage, that comes with being completely secure, and knowing your future.

I couldn't even imagine myself being like them. But here I was.

It was halfway through maths when the command came from on high. Mr Stainsby, in the Head's absence, issued a statement to be read out in every class. "Any students who witnessed the tragic incident in the park this morning should attend specially arranged trauma counselling in the upper school hall during the lunch break. An officer from the local police will also be on hand, if any student has information they would like to bring forward. The police officer will not, repeat not, be answering questions relating to the incident. It has come to the staff's attention that a small number of students took photographs at the scene using their phones, and that some of these photographs are now circulating around the school. These photographs are to be deleted immediately. The school has been advised that students may be committing an offence by storing them, uploading them to a social-networking website, or sending them to others."

The murder was more or less the only topic of conversation outside lessons. By lunchtime, Chinese whispers had included everything in the story from a pack of wild dogs to a carful of drug dealers. The one consistent thing, the one thing everyone appeared to agree on, was that at the root of it all was the Elton Gardens estate. No doubt about it. That was where these things started, definitely, no question. Bet it was gangs.

Being the new kid, I didn't like to butt in. I had plenty to say about the fact that the corpse had obviously been dissected with care, and certainly not gunned down in a drive-by shooting. I also had plenty to say about sweeping generalizations and appalling prejudices. I said none of it.

I did make a few guarded comments to Liam. We got talking a bit more after maths, mostly about the homework we'd been given, which was on a topic I'd never even heard of, let alone studied. I surmised that he was the class expert on science and technical subjects.

When the bell for lunch break went, Liam and I joined the long queue in the canteen. I'd expected to be able to find somewhere quiet to eat my sandwiches in peace, but absolutely nobody appeared to have brought a packed lunch with them, so I left my lunchbox at the bottom of my bag and stood in line for pie and chips.

"They given you a pre-pay card yet?" said Liam.

"No, I've got some cash," I said, as casually as I could. Luckily, I'd taken a fiver from my wallet before leaving home. I just hoped pie and chips wouldn't come to more than that!

The canteen was the standard model: the trailing queue, dinner ladies clanking their pots behind enormous metal serving units, rigidly arranged tables and chairs. A few minutes later – £4.20, phew – we weaved our way across the room with our plastic trays. Liam made a beeline for a small table in the corner where a girl was already sitting. She nodded a hello as Liam and I approached. The table was meant for two, but Liam found a spare chair and I squeezed in awkwardly at the side, pulling the chair as far forward as I could, so I didn't stick out too much. Our three trays took up about a hundred and twenty per cent of the available table space.

"This is Jo," said Liam. He pointed at me. "This is Sam Hunter, new today, Marlo's class."

"Hello," smiled Jo. She was moon-faced and freckly, with a mass of messy curls. She and Liam had the same date of birth, they later told me, which was how they'd originally got talking.

"Hi," I smiled. I had no idea what to say next.

"How are you finding this place?" said Jo.

"Er, different," I said, with raised eyebrows. "It looks like I've got some catching up to do."

"Yeah, they said that to a girl in my class," said Jo. "She's new this year, too, and she seems fine. I wouldn't worry."

Liam was already halfway through his pie. "I wish someone would send me one of those murder pictures," he said, through a mouthful. "Have you two seen any?"

"No," said Jo. "Fat Matt in our class said he was there, but that's crap."

"I was there," I said.

They both gazed at me. A morsel of pie was poised on Liam's bottom lip. "Really?" he said.

"Really," I said.

"You lucky sod," grumbled Liam. "The most interesting thing that's happened in ages and I missed it."

"It's no joke," I said. "I really don't think you'd want to see any pictures. It was horrible."

"Are you OK about it?" said Jo. "I saw a few people going into the upper school hall a minute ago."

"I'm fine, weirdly enough. I think I'm still a bit shell-shocked. It keeps popping into my head, though. And nobody around here seems too surprised... I mean, no offence, but except for those who saw it, people seem to have your attitude to it."

"None taken," grinned Jo. "Sorry, we're not being jokey, it's just, y'know, Elton Gardens. There's *always* stuff going on over there."

I had to say something. "It clearly wasn't gangs, or anything like that. The poor guy was deliberately cut up."

Liam edged forward slightly. "Is it true his head was chopped off?"

I hesitated. "Not really... The top half was. That's what I mean – he was cold-bloodedly opened up, he wasn't beaten or shot or anything."

"Even so," said Jo, "Elton Gardens really has got a terrible reputation. Honestly, I wouldn't put anything past them. Actual murders are pretty rare, I admit, so this is serious shit. They found a garage full of ketamine the other week and they found an arm in the river about a year ago. It's like Gotham City!"

"An arm?" I said. "On its own?"

"Yup, no body, nothing. Severed arm, sliced clean off. It was pumped full of drugs, too. Medical stuff, I mean, not Class As. They kept those sort of gory details out of the press, for some reason."

"How do you know about it?" I said.

"My dad's a journalist on the *Hadlington Courier*," said Jo. "So I get to hear all kinds of good stuff."

"Really?" I said. I unintentionally blurted my enthusiasm. "Would they be interested in an article? By me, I mean. About what I saw? I'm thinking about a career in journalism." I don't know what made me say it. I wouldn't have, normally.

"Yeah?" said Jo. "Well, I can ask. They don't usually take much stuff from freelancers, but you never know. If not, when we get to Work Experience week, I can definitely get you into Dad's office."

"That'd be brilliant!" I beamed.

"What do your parents do?" said Liam.

My stomach suddenly turned inside out but I tried not to let anything show on my face. "Er, my mum works in a bank, and my dad ... has his own business."

I knew for a fact they'd been assuming that Mum was a branch manager and Dad was some sort of suited entrepreneur. Embarrassment clawed at my guts.

"Are you two, er...?" I said, swinging a hand between Liam and Jo.

Jo blinked at me. "What? No! No, just mates," she laughed.

"Just mates," said Liam, a touch less earnestly. He'd finished his pie and chips.

"We're both complete nerds," said Jo. "We both love comics and old sci-fi movies and the same TV."

"Really?" I said. I admitted to my own nerdiness at once.

"Nooooo," grinned Jo. "We're *three* nerds! Yay! What are your favourite comics?"

"*Watchmen*."

"Ding!" declared Liam, striking an invisible mid-air bell. "And?"

"Early *Spider-Man*, Ditko and Romita."

"Ding!"

We chatted enthusiastically, the rest of the room and the morning fading away behind me. It turned out that Jo even drew comics of her own.

"She's the school's top artist," said Liam, holding

his gaze on her. "Have you seen the painting near Stainsby's office?"

"The big one?" I said. "On the stairs, pop art that looks like a Roy Lichtenstein?"

"That's Jo's," said Liam. She blushed and returned his gaze.

"Wow," I said. "It reminded me of that one of his with the drowning girl."

"Liam can't draw, but then I can't do science," said Jo. "Did he tell you he's got a lab at home?"

"A lab?"

"In the garage," said Liam. "I experiment with making electronic gadgets. I started with a couple of kits I got ages ago, but I make my own from scratch now. Are you doing electronics and DT?"

"No, they clashed with English lit and politics, so I'm doing those."

I was beginning to suspect that everyone at this school had something brilliantly impressive in their CV. How the hell was I ever going to measure up?

It was at that moment that a subtle ripple ran through the canteen. You know when you get an odd sense that someone significant has walked into the room? Maybe it's the combined effect of everyone suddenly taking notice of someone. Or maybe it's more psychological, something in the collective subconscious, if you happen to believe in that sort of thing. I suppose some people have a presence. One of them was the girl who was now in the dinner queue.

On any number of websites, you'll see pictures of the most attractive women on the planet — film stars, pop stars, models. Even at first glance, this girl made every last one of them look like a tired old hag. You didn't want to blink, in case you missed a single millisecond of her.

She was athletic, but not obviously sporty; graceful, but not fragile; vibrant, but not flashy. She was smoothly sculptured, with an elegantly contoured face and large bluey-grey eyes. A gentle flow of russet hair fell about her shoulders. As she talked to the friend standing next to her in the queue, her smile seemed to radiate across the room. She was exquisite, extraordinary.

Liam's face was suddenly beside mine. I think I must have been staring.

"That," said Liam quietly, trying to suppress a grin, "is Emma Greenhill." He sat back, giving me a look that seemed to suggest that this was all anyone needed to know.

"Miss Perfect," muttered Jo, with a caustic edge to her voice as she watched the girl over her shoulder. "Academically excellent, good at the piano, star of the hockey team, large circle of friends, a hit in the school plays, obvious candidate for Most Popular Girl In The School."

"Yeah, she seems nice," I said, as off the cuff as possible. Liam smirked to himself.

"She is nice," said Jo, with a sigh. "Genuinely kind and thoughtful. Makes you sick."

I suppose it was unthinking bravado that made me say: "Does she have a boyfriend?"

"Believe it or not, no," said Liam. "I always get the impression she's not interested."

"Oh," I said. "Does that mean she's...?"

"No, she's not," said Jo. "She's just too busy being cool to bother. Dedicated to being completely great. Come on, have we finished?"

She stood up. Liam and I followed her across to put away our plates. Then, on our way out, we walked right behind the queue.

Emma Greenhill was being glared at by the

dinner lady at the till.

"Sorry, can't I owe it?" said Emma.

"You know that's against the rules. Another 80p, or put it all back." The woman was all hairnet and housecoat, with a scowl in between. Emma's friend, behind her, was rummaging in her bag.

I'd acted almost before I thought about it. I dug into my pocket for my change, and dropped the coins into the dinner lady's hand. "There you are."

Emma turned. Her beautiful face shone at me. "Thank you," she said. "Are you sure?"

"Of course," I smiled. Wow, I was so smooth.

"That's very kind of you," said Emma. "I'll pay you back tomorrow."

"No need," I said. "What's 80p?"

She laughed. A sound like the singing of an angel.

"You going to stand there talking all day now?" grunted the dinner lady.

Emma moved aside. Her focus was still on me. "Well, thank you. I had a bit of a late night, and forgot my card. I should carry more change. Sorry, I don't know your name."

"I'm Sam," I said. "Sam Hunter." Bond, James Bond.

"Nice to meet you, Sam-Sam Hunter. See you around."

"See you," I smiled.

Ding!

I didn't dare look back. Liam scurried up to me outside the canteen.

"That was cool," he declared. "She was totally flirting with you!"

"What? Really?"

"She was doing the curling her hair with her finger thing," spluttered Liam.

"Was she?" I said, frowning.

"I can see you're a hit with the lay-deez," he went on, jabbing me in the ribs.

"Actually, no, never," I said, feeling a little unsteady. "But I was cool, wasn't I?"

"You were. You were."

I took a deep breath. This had to be the weirdest day of my life.

"Where does she live?" I asked.

"Emma? Oh, just down the road," said Liam. "There's a little cul de sac called Priory Mews. She lives in this whacking great mansion – her family is loaded. Bierce Priory, that's the place."

I told him my new address.

"You," said Liam slowly. "Live. Next door. To Emma Greenhill?"

"Apparently."

Chapter Three

I had separate lessons to Liam after lunch. The afternoon seemed to go by in a blur. English with Miss Marlo was OK, but the group I was in for politics were nothing but braying snobs. I kept myself to myself.

When the bell went for the end of the school day, I felt an immense sense of relief. It was only then that I realized how tense I'd been.

The school gradually exhaled its pupils. Jo waved as she sped ahead of me on her bike and, coming back out on to Maybrick Road, Liam caught up with me.

"Do you think the police are still down there?" he asked, nodding towards the path across the road.

I could see where this was going. "Probably not. I expect they've got everything they need and gone."

"Show me the spot, then," said Liam.

I sighed wearily. "Do I have to?"

"Yeeeah, go on, I'm interested."

"You're sick."

"Come on, they'll have cleaned up all the blood. I just want to see where it happened."

I shrugged and followed him. The sky was glowering overhead, with heavy clouds drifting slowly and darkly over the town, the daylight already fading.

I was wrong. The police were still tramping around in white coveralls. A plastic tent had been put up over the crime scene. I got the impression that they were close to leaving, however, because equipment was being packed into black zip-up bags. A large police van was parked where the car had been that morning. We turned round and went back the way we'd come.

"Not my day, is it," grumbled Liam. "Oh well, see you tomorrow."

He trudged off in the opposite direction to me, his tall, angular figure loping along. He lived at the far end of Maybrick Road, close to the point where the River Arvan ran under the stone road bridge we'd driven over on our drive around town the day before.

I kept an eye out for Emma all the way home,

but didn't see her. I guessed she was staying late at school, doing something extra-curricular.

As I walked into Priory Mews, I could see Mum and Dad chatting with the neighbours. The ones from Nos. 1 and 2, that is, not Emma Greenhill. There was the old couple I'd seen Dad talking to the day before, and a much younger couple, with a wriggling toddler in the man's arms.

A delivery van was parked outside our house. A tightly shrinkwrapped washing machine was being unloaded on to a battered trolley by the driver.

Mum spotted me as she signed for it. "Hello – good day at the new school?" she chirped.

"Not bad," I said. "What are you doing home this early?"

"Induction day. I finished at dinner time." She all but dragged me over to the neighbours. I was impatient to write the article I'd mentioned to Jo, and email it over to her, but Mum insisted. "Everyone, this is Sam. He's started at Maybrick High today." She said it as if she was saying 'Eton' or 'Cambridge University'.

"Hi," I said weakly.

The old couple from No. 2 were Mr and Mrs

Gifford. They were both short and wore fawn cardigans which, while not actually matching, definitely looked like they'd been bought in the same shop. Mr Gifford was beaky and peering, with a neat green collar and tie. Mrs Gifford spent the whole time delicately holding the lowest bead of her necklace. Both of them had the same very slightly runny nose, a single thin line of yellow visible on their upper lips. Mrs Gifford dabbed hers with a hanky. Mr Gifford sniffed.

The people from No. 1 were the Daltons. Michael, Susan and their two-year-old Greye. With an 'e'. Greye, for God's sake! The child wriggled and whined. His multi-coloured socks dangled off the ends of his pudgy feet.

"Are you cold, sweets?" cooed his mother. "Daddy get you your coat."

Mum flashed the sunny face at me she reserved for social situations. "Did you make some new friends today?" she said. And to make it worse, she added an aside to the neighbours. "He finds it difficult to make new friends. We've moved around a lot."

"Yes, they do these days," smiled Mr Gifford. That didn't make any sense, did it? He nodded sagely, and Mrs Gifford nodded sagely, too.

I wanted to die. Greye whined.

"Has Daddy not got you your coat yet, sweets?"

Without a word, Daddy handed the child to Mummy and headed back into their house.

"Sam?" prompted Mum.

"Er, yes, I made a couple of friends," I said, in a smart-alec tone. "I met the girl who lives over there." I indicated the Priory.

"Oh, Emma," smiled Mrs Gifford.

"Emma," said Susan Dalton. "She's a lovely girl, isn't she?"

"Lovely girl," agreed Mrs Gifford.

Susan Dalton dabbled at Greye's rosy cheeks. "She's your favourite babysitter, isn't she?"

"They're a lovely family," smiled Mrs Gifford.

"Pillars of the community," added Mr Gifford. "Emma's father, Byron Greenhill, is a surgeon. Or was. I believe he's in research now. One of the country's leading psychopharmacologists."

"Crikey, there's a word with a big Scrabble score!" said Dad.

Mum laughed a little too loudly.

Michael Dalton came back holding a chunky

little anorak that Greye kicked and grumbled over while it was put on him.

"There you go, sweets," said Susan. "Daddy get your tea ready in a minute." They both smiled amiably at their squirming little brat, then at the rest of us.

"And Byron's father lives at the Priory, too," smiled Mrs Gifford.

"Solid fellow, Ken Greenhill," smiled Mr Gifford. "Served over thirty-five years on the town council. Half the amenities in this area are his doing. Very sound fellow. The Greenhills are a very respected family. The library up in town is reopening soon, saved from closure and fully refurbished by the Greenhills."

"How marvellous," said Mum.

"Pillars of the community," repeated Mr Gifford. "Byron's brother is the local chief constable, and I believe they have relatives in Whitehall. A couple of senior civil servants, and one is in Parliament."

"An MP, yes," smiled Mrs Gifford.

"I might pop over later and say hi," said Dad.

No, please don't, I groaned inwardly.

"The Greenhills' annual Halloween Ball is the

49

social event of the year," smiled Michael Dalton. "That's where I met Susan."

Susan bobbed a finger on Greye's nose. "That's where Mummy met Daddy."

I was beginning to feel slightly creeped out by these people. I couldn't quite put my finger on why.

"Is there a Mrs Greenhill?" said Mum.

"Oh, yes, Caroline," smiled Mrs Gifford. "She's our local GP. Wonderful doctor."

"She delivered you, didn't she, sweets?" burbled Susan.

"Caroline Greenhill?" said Dad. "I know that name from somewhere."

"She was on the television a few years ago," smiled Mr Gifford. "One of those medical advisers, sitting on a sofa and answering viewers' queries."

"Oh, yes!" declared Dad. "I remember. On that morning thing on ITV. Good-looking woman. Well, well, two celebs in the same street."

He meant himself. He actually meant himself.

The van driver emerged from our house. "You're plumbed in. All set."

"Thank you," said Mum, as if she was about to add "my good man" at the end. Immediately, you could tell she wanted to go and play with her new toy. "Well, I'm so glad we've met you all. We'd better let you get on."

Greye wriggled and griped. "Has Daddy not got your tea ready yet?" said Susan.

It was only as she said it that I noticed something about her and Michael. Both of them had the same slightly runny nose as Mr and Mrs Gifford, a thin yellow reflection off their top lips. Michael wiped at his with a crumpled handkerchief as they went back indoors.

Eurgh, I thought. *Some bug going round.*

Inside our house, I almost tripped over the seven rolls of carpet that were laid along the hallway, all of them wound in plastic sheeting. New carpet smell was even better than new car smell.

"Don't tread on them!" cried Mum, hearing the crinkling of the plastic from the kitchen. "The fitter's coming in the morning."

"Which one is for my room?" I called.

"You said you wanted dark blue, kiddo," said Dad, pottering about in the living room. "You got dark blue."

"Thanks!"

As I dropped my school bag underneath the coat hooks in the hall, and hung up my blazer, the letter box clattered and a newspaper dropped on to the floor.

I picked the paper up. Not the one Jo's dad worked on. This was one of those thin advertising freesheets. The headline on the front said 'Runaway Girl: No Contact'. Beside a slightly fuzzy picture of a teenager was a breathless report in tabloid-speak about a nineteen-year-old from Elton Gardens who'd gone on the run from her drug-dealing boyfriend. Her family hadn't heard from her since she'd vanished overnight the previous week.

I frowned at it. *Was that murder a gang killing after all?* I thought. Everyone at school was so sure about it. It *was* possible that I was mistaken, wasn't it? Perhaps there were just some very strange and nasty gangs in this part of the world…? I chucked the paper on to the small table beside the coat hooks.

Looking back, I was too ready to take that report at face value. I was too ready to dismiss my own doubts, too willing to set aside the revulsion I'd felt at the snobbish attitudes of everyone around here to Elton Gardens. Believing that report fitted too neatly into the background information I'd need for my own article, the one for Jo's dad, the opportunity I wanted to grab.

If only I'd read between the lines. But we're all wise in hindsight, I guess.

Mum's voice came from the kitchen. "I've unpacked the microwave! Pasta or curry?"

Dad's voice came from the living room. "Curry!"

"Yes, curry!" I called.

We had pasta. I sat in my room until dinner was ready, tapping out my article. As soon as it was done, I emailed it to Jo, then sifted through the homework I'd been given. I tried to ignore the fact that my bed frame was still sitting untouched in the corner.

My mind kept wandering back over the events of the day. Once or twice I looked out of my window, across to the Priory, wondering if I might catch sight of Emma. It was hard to even imagine a girl like that living in such an austere place.

We ate in silence, apart from Dad's occasional humming, and a brief conversation about what we could do with the two smaller downstairs rooms. Mum suggested an extra guest room. Dad suggested a cinema room with a projector. I quite liked that idea. Then he suggested a room in which to display his music-industry memorabilia. So, basically, a room full of his useless junk. That idea, I was less keen on.

After a while, Mum piped up. "The neighbours seem very nice. Decent people."

Dad mmm-ed through his pasta.

"What do they all do, Mum?" I said.

"Mr Gifford was a solicitor, he said. I think Mrs Gifford said she did something at a shop? Anyway, they're both retired, obviously. The Daltons are very swish – he's an interior designer and she does websites."

I wrinkled up my nose. "Don't they all strike you as a bit … dopey?"

"What? No, of course they don't. Why do you have to think the worst of people?"

"They seem a bit odd, that's all," I said. "They don't stop smiling."

"What's wrong with being cheerful? Honestly, Sam."

"They creep me out a bit," I muttered.

Mum started clattering plates and clearing up. That was normally her wordless signal that I'd annoyed her. "They're our neighbours now, and they probably will be for years, and you can make sure you get on with them whether you like it or not," she said. She thought for a moment. "What's this Emma like, then? She sounds like a lovely girl."

"She's OK," I said.

"You want to keep in with her," said Mum. "It'd be good to get an invitation to that Halloween party the Daltons mentioned."

You could almost see pound signs in her eyes. Her approval of someone generally rose in direct proportion to their income. I'd been dragged to her work's Christmas thing the previous year, where she'd spent the evening laughing at nothing and telling me to ask the manager's daughter to dance.

"I fancy a good party," said Dad, in between swigs of beer. "Bloody hell, I live in the same street as that Doctor Caroline. Phhwooar."

I winced. Dad let out a long, low belch.

Mum frowned at him and tutted. "Richard!"

I suppose most people wonder what the hell their parents ever saw in each other. I'd often wondered why Mum put up with Dad's spendthrift habits, and his so-called collecting, especially when she could be such a cheapskate herself. I always got the impression that she was far from blind to his faults. Maybe, deep down, she was almost as much of a dreamer as he was. Maybe, years ago, she saw him as full of potential.

And then, all those years without progress, without success. I think she was disappointed with how things had turned out, but she kept on being supportive of him so she wouldn't be disappointed with him, too. She held on to the idea that he was one of those great undiscovered talents who'd never quite got a break. She nagged at him, sometimes relentlessly, but she never stopped believing in him. Of course, neither of them ever said anything of the sort to me. But, I guess, as you start to grow up, you start to see your parents as they really are. It's very unsettling.

Since the arrival of the massive song royalties, their relationship had definitely moved on. She wouldn't be moaning at him to get off his fat arse any more. Now they were too busy flashing each other loved-up glances. It was enough to make you heave.

To change the subject, I told them about my article. They seemed genuinely impressed, and it boosted my confidence that Jo's dad might actually get it in the paper.

I went to bed early. I settled down on the mattress, the glow from my lamp at my shoulder, listening to the soft rush of the central heating system. I tried reading for a while, but other thoughts kept demanding attention. Everything was churning around in my head. I remember thinking how bright the future seemed.

I didn't feel particularly tired, but I must have drifted off to sleep with the book flopped on my chest and the lamp still throwing grey mountain shadows on to the opposite wall.

I thought, at first, that I'd dreamed the blood-chilling scream that came from outside.

Chapter Four

It shook me like a slap in the face. It was some distance away, and heavily muffled by the double glazing, but it was so sharp, so filled with terror, that it cut into my mind like a razor blade. It was a howling shriek of pain.

I flinched, and my eyes popped open. I blinked and squinted in the sudden rush of light from my lamp. Fumbling, I switched it off.

What the hell was that?

I lay absolutely still. There was silence, not even the occasional ticking of the heating.

Lying there, in the calm and the darkness, I wondered if I could have dreamed it. Surely, a sound like that…? Was it one of those vivid dreams you have to consciously shrug off, one of those nightmare impressions that leaves you doubting that you're back in reality when you wake up? I wanted it to be a dream. After all, a scream in the dead of night was…

My sleep-fogged mind circled groggily around the idea of getting up to investigate. I twisted around on the mattress and looked over at the dim glow of my alarm clock. I'd put it over by the door, so that I couldn't roll over and switch it off in the mornings.

2:12 a.m. My heart was thumping. How long I lay there for, I don't know. Several minutes, at a guess. Not a single sound came from outside. With every passing moment, the urge to fling my duvet aside and rush to the window grew stronger. But, at the same time, the continuing silence fuelled my doubts.

Instinct told me that the scream was real. It had knocked me out of sleep. The only time such a thing had ever happened to me before was when a car windscreen had been broken down in the street below my bedroom, years ago. On the other hand, plain common sense said it was nothing but my own imagination.

What if…

Another murder? Like the body by the river? No, we were too far from the territory of any gangs for that to be the explanation. Elton Gardens was almost half a mile down the hill. The scream had been distant, a lot further away than the Giffords' house, or the Daltons', but it had still woken me. It had been distinct. It couldn't have come from anywhere near the river. It could only have come from the Priory.

I couldn't let it go. I couldn't hear something like that and not act. Someone had screamed for their life, someone…

…female. That was a female voice.

Emma! What if Emma was in danger?

I rubbed the last of the sleep from my eyes and quickly clambered to my feet. The room wasn't cold, but still a shock after the warmth of my bed. I rushed over to the window and peered out nervously. There was a very faint glint of light visible from the street lamps on Maybrick Road, largely obscured by the trees on the Priory's land. For the first time, it struck me that there was no street lighting in Priory Mews, none at all.

Call the police? More indecision clawed at me. No, if it *was* Emma who was in trouble, then even a slight delay could have terrible consequences. I had to act now! Fumbling in haste, I wrapped myself in my dressing gown and pulled on yesterday's socks.

I turned and hurried down to Mum and Dad's

room. The door was slightly ajar. A brief glimpse inside told me that they hadn't heard anything. They were dead to the world.

I said I would write this account as objectively as I could. That's what a responsible journalist would do. So, in the interests of objectivity, I must record, here and now, that the decision to leave my room that night was a profound mistake.

If only I'd woken my parents, if only I'd listened to the silence and my own doubts, if only I hadn't been in such a rush to do something heroic, then everything would have turned out differently. Leaving the house that night was the spark that lit the fuse. My suspicions would still have been aroused. I would still have asked questions, and investigated, and tried to find out where that scream had come from, but events would have unfolded in a very different way, and perhaps the worst of them might have been avoided.

The awful fact is, I wasn't thinking straight. It may be that I was still half asleep, I don't know. For whatever reason, it never even occurred to me that if it was indeed Emma who was in trouble, she had a household of adults around her to help. That one simple, obvious thought would have kept me in my room. I would have been very concerned, certainly, sleepless and even scared, but I wouldn't have been running for the front door.

However, the thought never entered my head. So that's that.

I ran downstairs, jammed on my school shoes and put my coat on over my dressing gown.

Cold night air pinched at me as I stepped outside. Priory Mews was as motionless as the corpse in the park. There was no far-off rumble of traffic. No stars were visible in the sky, the clouds were hanging as low and thick as they had the previous day.

I stood a few metres from my front door, watching, listening. I hugged my arms in tightly, but couldn't stop shivering. I tried to breathe as quietly as I could, straining my ears to pick up something, anything that might give me a clue about what to do now. My breath clouded around my face.

Gradually, my eyes were becoming accustomed to the dark. The outlines of my house, and of the Giffords' and the Daltons', were slowly filled in with grey-on-grey details. I could see the road surface beneath my shoes.

Our neighbours' homes were in complete darkness. Their sleep hadn't been broken either.

Taking delicate steps, I walked around to the side of our house, on to the grassy area beside our garden gate, heading for the Priory. I had to move slowly, even on the grass, because I still wasn't sure of the exact layout.

The large rear garden of Bierce Priory was surrounded by a very tall, black wrought-iron fence. At the side, a narrow padlocked gate led on to the steep hill overlooking the park, and the path down to the river.

I stepped stealthily along by the railings. They were too closely placed for anyone to squeeze through, and too high to climb without help.

I stood motionless again, shivering a little less as I acclimatized to the chill of the night. From there, I could just about make out the Priory's looming shape. It rose up into the sky like jagged teeth.

I watched and waited but heard nothing, saw nothing. I began to doubt myself again. Perhaps there was nothing to hear other than the sped-up beating of my own heart, and the throb of blood through my ears. Then … I did hear something.

A gasping sound. A sort of agonized panting. And a slight rustling, like feet tramping slowly through long grass.

I felt as if my heart would stop. I reached out and gripped the freezing cold-railings with both hands. The sounds were definitely coming from the grounds of the Priory. Somewhere over to the left. They seemed to be moving away from the building. Towards me.

I screwed up my face, willing my eyes to pick out something I could identify. The gasping sound was getting closer. It seemed almost like sobbing now, like pain and terror crushed down into exhaustion.

Movement!

I caught sight of a shape. Low, close to the ground, moving slowly towards the fence.

Was it someone crawling? I gripped the bars tighter, pulling my face close to them. I couldn't make sense of the shape for a moment.

It was a dog. Quite a large one. Its head was bent, lolling forward.

I suddenly let my breath go. Just a dog, for God's sake, probably out for a late-night sniff around the garden.

But then, as I watched it, my heart seized up once more. As it moved closer I could see it was pulling itself along. Unsteadily, slowly, shaking with effort. At least one of its hind legs was dragging on the grass. The poor creature was obviously in dreadful pain.

I was about to speak. I was about to crouch down, and put out my hand through the bars. Suddenly, I almost let out a gasp of shock, as the dog was pulled back into the darkness.

In a flash, it was gone! It let out a brief, feeble yelp of fright, and then there was silence once more.

Terror froze me to the spot. I'd heard nothing else, I'd heard nobody approaching. I caught a brief glimpse of a figure, quite tall, scooping the dog up in its arms. My hands were gripping the railings so tightly that my fingers hurt. I couldn't utter a sound. I wanted to shout out at whoever it was. I wanted to yell at them to stop, but my chest felt as if there was an immense weight pressing down on it, and I simply couldn't form the words.

An intruder? Had someone got into the garden, over the fence, from the park?

A dozen possibilities ran through my head. Of all

of them, the most likely seemed to be the relatively innocent one, that someone had been walking their dog through the park. It had run off, been injured by something, and slipped through the railings into the Priory's grounds. Its owner had climbed over the fence to retrieve the animal.

Was that the source of the scream? Half asleep, had I mistaken the high-pitched sound of the dog's cries for a woman's scream?

For a moment, I was almost reassured. This seemed a logical explanation. If, that is, I set aside the oddity of someone taking their pet for a walk at two in the morning, and the creepiness of their snatching it up like that, not to mention the presence of some hazard in the park sufficient to badly injure a large dog in the first place. Yes, that was the logical explanation.

I'll tell Emma in the morning, I thought. *There was someone in your garden last night.* I'd tell her I saw it all from my window, and hope she wouldn't realize how impossibly good my eyesight must have been. Had she been woken by that dreadful sound the poor dog made? *Yes, perhaps you should install some of those motion-sensitive security lights; you can't be too careful.*

Just as I was calming myself down with the full

story, I caught another momentary glimpse of the tall figure.

It wasn't heading away, back to the park. It was striding towards the Priory.

I could hear footsteps clearly now, swishing against the grass. Its outline was bulky, the limp form of the dog hanging out to either side. The figure faded into the darkness. Seconds later, I heard a clicking sound coming from the direction of the Priory. A key in a lock?

Not a dog walker, and not an intruder. Someone from the Priory itself.

Whoever it was hadn't seen me. They can't have, or they'd have said something, or done something. They wouldn't just turn and walk back, not when they'd obviously crept up behind the dog so stealthily. No, they couldn't have seen me.

My heart was running like a steam engine. Who the hell had that been? Had the scream been the dog, then? What was going on?

I couldn't hold my breathing back any longer. Mist fogged around my face, the night air rasping at my throat and lungs. I was shivering even more now, from cold and from horror.

At least they hadn't seen me.

I felt my way back along the fence, holding on to the railings just to stop my hands trembling. I could feel the dampness of the grass soaking into the sides of my socks and the hems of my pyjamas.

I wanted to run. Back home, into my bed, under the covers, into oblivion.

I don't know what made me look up at that moment. It might have been some confused effort to find clues as to what was going on with the dog. Perhaps it was a sixth sense, warning me. Whatever made me do it, I wish I hadn't.

There was a single light on in the Priory. Way up, at one of the top-floor windows. It was faint, shadowy and yellowish, the illumination of a small table lamp or a wall light.

My blood turned cold and my stomach knotted.

There was a face at the window.

It was peculiar and distorted; a strange, twisted grimace that seemed to float in the shadows. It was narrow but its actual shape was indistinct, a horrible shifting mix of darkness and flesh. I was fully fifteen metres away, but I had an impression of age, of folds and lines, pale sunken cheeks.

I was transfixed, because it was staring at me. Directly at me, with mad eyes that seemed to ask who I was, why I was there. For long seconds, the face stared into mine.

And then it grinned. Toothy and insane. It nodded at me, in greeting.

My nerve snapped. I ran.

I slammed the front door behind me, shaking with fright and gasping for breath. I kicked off my shoes, wrenched off my coat and ran back upstairs.

Mum and Dad were still asleep. Not even the bump of the door or the thudding of my feet on the stairs had disturbed them.

I retreated to my room, pulling the covers over me and shutting my eyes so tightly it made them sting. I tried to blank my mind and think of something nice, or think of anything but the dog, and the figure, and the face.

I tried to piece it all together, but my nerves were too jangled for rational analysis. How had the dog got hurt? Why had the figure grabbed it like that? Whose face had that been?

I thought back to what Mr Gifford next door had said about the Greenhills. The face was too old to be

Emma's mother, it certainly wasn't Emma herself, and it was definitely no kind of mask. It had moved, it was alive, I was sure of that. There was someone living there Mr Gifford hadn't mentioned, that was all. Simple as that. Some elderly relative.

Who had seen me. The figure in the garden hadn't, but the face upstairs had.

And who was the figure? Too tall for Emma. One of her parents?

What about the scream that started it all?

I lay in bed, trying to calm down. I struggled to rid myself of the slithering fear that something was coming up the stairs to get me. I couldn't make sense of it all. At that moment, I didn't want to.

Looking back, I guess even then I could have walked away. Ignored it, put it down to a mixture of misinterpretation and an overactive imagination fuelled by all the fiction I'd read and watched. I could have told myself it was none of my business, nothing to do with me, somebody else's problem. People say that to themselves every day, don't they? Turn a blind eye… Hide things away, even from themselves… The elephant in the room.

How I ever slept, I'll never know. I must have

blanked out a couple of hours later from complete exhaustion. The next thing I remember was waking up with daylight on my face.

I wriggled over to squint at the clock. It was twenty past eight – I must have slept right through the alarm. If I didn't hurry, I'd be late for school.

Jumping up, I checked the view from my window. Bierce Priory looked exactly the same as usual, silent and glowering. A large silver people carrier, a Renault, was sitting on the drive. There was no sign of movement in the house, no faces at any windows. Complete normality.

I hurried into my bathroom. Ten minutes later, I clattered downstairs.

Mum hadn't left for work yet. She was standing in the hall, talking to a tall woman who was wearing an elegantly cut business suit. The woman had a refined, carefully made-up face, with high cheekbones and a smart black bob.

"Oh, here he is," chirped Mum, "running late. Come and say hello, Sam."

My face must have betrayed a certain wariness. The woman stepped forward and held out her hand to shake. It felt cold and soft, like a recently killed

71

fish. I'd guessed who she was before she said a word.

"Hello, Sam, I'm Doctor Greenhill," she said in a voice like warm chocolate. "My daughter Emma mentioned she'd met you."

"Yes," I said feebly. Did she know I'd been seen last night? Did she know I knew about the dog?

"I was just saying to your mother," she continued, "I'm so sorry we couldn't come over and introduce ourselves yesterday. My husband had a function to attend last night. It's so nice to have new neighbours."

"Doctor Greenhill says she'll take us on as patients at her surgery," chirruped Mum. "Isn't that lovely?"

Caroline Greenhill shot a glance at Mum. The air of amused condescension on Dr Greenhill's face made me want to crawl under a stone with embarrassment. Mum was giving me one of her 'go on, speak up' looks.

"I like to have a good chat with my new patients, individually," said Dr Greenhill. "I've made appointments for all three of you at the surgery. Yours is immediately after school today, Sam, all right?"

It was such a straightforward statement, so casually said, and so apparently helpful and caring.

It would take me weeks to realize its full meaning.

I might easily have fallen into the trap, but luckily the night's events had put me on my guard. I wanted to keep my distance from the Priory's inhabitants, at least for the moment, until I could make some sort of sense out of what I'd seen. I chose my words with care.

"I'm fine," I said in a low voice. "There's nothing wrong with me."

"Just a chat." Dr Greenhill smiled.

"Just a chat." Mum smiled.

"I may have to stay late tonight," I said. "There's work I have to catch up on."

"I'm sure you can catch up later. Your mother's been telling me what a bright boy you are. I'll expect you at three forty-five."

I felt a sudden flush of defiance. "I suppose I have been feeling a bit tired," I said.

"Yes?" said Dr Greenhill. Her head tipped to one side a little.

"Yes, I didn't get much sleep last night. I heard noises. Strange noises."

"We didn't," said Mum. "What noises?"

"In the middle of the night," I said.

"I'm afraid our household tends to turn in early," said Dr Greenhill. "We're all out like lights. Oh, perhaps you heard our old boiler? The pipes make some dreadful screeches and squeals but we don't even notice it any more. I'm so sorry if it woke you, it can get horribly loud. We really must have it repaired!" She turned to Mum. "I mustn't keep you any longer, Ellen. You'll be late for work."

"No problem, they can wait for me for once," she laughed, a little too much. "I'll tell Richard about his appointment. He'll be terribly sorry he missed you."

"Until later, then," said Dr Greenhill. "I'll see you at three forty-five, Sam."

Mum waved at her from the front step as she crossed the street. A blast of cold air whipped into the hallway before Mum came inside.

"Don't forget that appointment, Sam," she said, gathering up her stuff for work.

"I'm not going," I said firmly.

"Don't be silly," said Mum mildly. "Of course you should go. I'm going in my lunch hour. It's very nice of Doctor Greenhill to fit us all in like that. I'm sure she's very busy."

"It was a scream I heard last night, Mum."

"You'll hear me scream if you miss that appointment."

"Seriously! Someone over in that house screamed!"

"You heard what she said," said Mum. "It's their pipes. I think if someone had actually screamed, Doctor Greenhill would have noticed, don't you?"

"I think she did notice," I said. "She must have noticed. I never said anything about a scream to her, I just said I'd heard a strange noise, and yet she came out with that crap about screeching pipes. As if she knew she needed a cover story. And I never said it was the Priory I heard it come from. She just assumed. She's hiding something. I don't know what, but something was going on over there last night. I went out to have a look, and—"

"What? You went out in the night?"

"Yes! To find out who screamed."

"And did you?"

"No, but there was an injured dog in the Priory grounds. Someone from the house took it back inside."

"Well, it was the dog that made the noise, then, obviously. Dogs do howl, you know, especially if they're injured. Oh, the poor thing! Doctor Greenhill didn't mention it."

"Which is also suspicious," I said. "If your dog hurt itself, why wouldn't you just say so? Why make up rubbish about heating pipes? Something was going on over there! And someone was at the window, I saw—"

Mum shook her head. "I've got to get to work, Sam."

"Aren't you listening to me?"

She turned to face me calmly. "Yes, I'm listening, Sam," she said softly. "You're speaking very loud."

I walked up to her. "I'm sorry, but—"

"Now I've got to go. I'll see you later. Have a nice day."

She headed out to the car.

Chapter Five

As soon as I arrived at my classroom that morning, I got Liam on his own and told him about what had happened. He snorted and pulled faces all the way through what I was saying.

"Is this a wind-up?"

"No," I said wearily, the fatigue of an almost sleepless night already starting to catch up with me.

"Because if you're interested in wind-ups, you're never going to beat Mad Maxwell in 11B. He convinced the staff he had a disease. They were raising funds. *And* he pulled an Ofsted scam on the school office. He's a comedy genius."

"Look, I know it sounds unlikely," I said, "but I promise you. There was a scream, there was a dog, there was a face. It frightened the crap out of me. I don't know who screamed, I don't know what happened to the dog, I don't know who the face was."

Liam eyed me silently for a moment or two. I could tell he was asking himself whether this new kid was a pathological liar or just a bit weird.

"I don't know what to think," I said. "That's why I'm telling you this. All I know is, last night happened, and this morning I've had a conversation with Emma's mother that convinces me she's got something to hide. I swear to you it's true. I've got more than enough on my plate right now, haven't I? Moving, new school, blah blah. Do you really think I'm going to start making things up on top of everything else?"

Liam shrugged. "I guess not. But … come on. Are you saying Emma Greenhill let out a blood-curdling scream at two in the morning? Why?"

"I don't even know for sure if it was her who screamed," I muttered. "But, assuming it was, then either she was in some sort of danger, or something scared the shit out of her. Have you seen her this morning?"

"Emma? I have, actually. She was coming along Maybrick Road at about the same time as me."

"And?"

"And what? She looks completely normal. Exactly

the same today as she always looks. Fabulous. What, did you expect her to have been chopped into pieces by a homicidal axeman?"

I sighed and rubbed my eyes. "You don't believe me, do you?"

He pulled another face. "It's not that, exactly. It's just... I'm not saying you're making it up or even imagining it. But there's got to be a simple explanation. What's that thing about a blade...? We did it in PSHE. Occam's Razor, that's it! Doesn't that say that the simplest solution is probably right? Well, the simplest solution is that the Greenhills have got a dog that howled like hell last night, because it got badly hurt, which was probably because of something one of them did, since today they don't want to talk about it, or even admit to it. Maybe Emma's dad is a secret drunk, and gave the dog a kicking? Ooooor, alternatively, if you insist on it being a human scream, Emma heard a row, came down, saw what had happened to the dog, and let rip. Her mum's embarrassed, so she made up a story about pipes in a panic, when she knew someone had heard a noise. There you are."

I shrugged. "And what about the face at the window?"

"Granny's staying, hears the commotion, wakes up, looks out. Simples. But if you ask me, there probably wasn't any face at all. People see faces and patterns in things all the time. There's that hill they photographed on Mars, isn't there, that people swear looks like an alien. We're biologically programmed to fit things together into shapes we understand. You said the light in the window was faint. Add a few reflections of objects inside, plus your own trouser-filling fear, and bingo, one terrifying apparition."

"Whoever snatched the dog away wasn't drunk," I said.

"OK, maybe someone's just a vicious bastard, and gave the dog a kicking when it chewed up a pair of slippers. Either way, Emma's mum might want to hush it up, right?"

"I dunno," I muttered. "You weren't there. You didn't hear that scream."

Liam did an exaggerated flop on to the nearest desk. "Saaaam. Look, you said yourself you were scared, right? What if half of what you saw, or heard, didn't actually happen as you think it did? Like when they say eyewitnesses at a violent crime scene all give different accounts of what they saw.

Stress causes people to remember stuff in totally different ways. I bet if we went and asked the kids who saw that dead body in the park to describe it in detail today, you'd end up with a dozen different descriptions, not one of them matching another. Bet you."

I thought about it. "Yes, I suppose that's true," I said. I thought about it some more. "But surely I'm not so stressed I'd misremember a scream or that face?"

Liam threw his arms wide. "Moving house, new school, tum-de-tum! Doctor Liam will see you now! Sam is a psycho-criminal maaaadman, it's official!" He boggled his eyes and lolled out his tongue.

Is Liam right? I thought. Were there other, simpler possibilities? Could I have just heard the howl of a fox, for example? Or a night-time yell from the Daltons' toddler? The squeals a toddler makes can be ear-splitting. Could the sound have morphed, in my sleep-filled mind, into a piercing scream? If so, then was what I saw at the Priory even connected to the sound? Was it simply a coincidence? Had I merely been in the right place at the right time to witness the kind of nasty but commonplace scenario

Liam was talking about? And couldn't my own fear have changed an ordinary face, looking out into the night – or an illusion of shadows and lines – into something sinister and frightening?

Liam's off-the-cuff explanation seemed perfectly plausible. Something had happened to the dog. The scream was either the dog, or someone's reaction to it. Emma's mum didn't want to admit to the truth. The face, if there'd been a face at all, was someone woken by the disturbance.

At the end of all this tortuous theorizing, I was still left with the same uncomfortable suspicion. No matter what the correct explanation of what had happened the previous night, it seemed to be the case that Emma Greenhill lived in a house where there was at least one unpleasant secret. And where there was one unpleasant secret, there would almost certainly be others.

At that moment, Miss Marlo came bustling in. Then it was registration, and then it was geography, and then it was English, and then it was break.

I met up with Liam again. He was sitting on the low wall outside the science block. It was a general meeting spot, with kids from various year groups squashed together all the way along the length of the wall, the older ones dominating the sunny spots.

Jo was with him, nibbling at one of those oatmeal bars that taste of cardboard. She announced, blushing, that she'd uploaded her latest comic book art to the blog she kept. We took a quick look on my phone: it was the third chapter of a detective story called *Bullet-train*.

It was pretty good. The artwork was quite sparse, but it didn't have that uncertain look about it, that slight distortion that shouts out that it's been done by a kid.

"The story's just basic," she said. "It's only meant as a showcase for the pictures, really."

"Well, it's very impressive," I said, and meant it.

"Don't you have a blog yourself?" said Jo. "If you're an aspiring journalist?"

The true answer to that question was that I'd started one many months before. I'd been too hesitant and too doubtful of my abilities to keep it going. I'd never felt I had anything interesting to say, and finally I'd deleted it in frustration.

"I've not found the time," I said, feeling my cheeks redden. "Too busy with school."

I think she sensed the truth. She pursed her lips slightly. "Umm, on the subject of journalism, have you checked your email?"

I hadn't. I tapped at my phone with a surging sense of excitement. There was a note from her dad, thanking me for the article, and turning it down. "Nicely written, but the descriptions are a little flowery, and also overall too graphic for us, I'm afraid. Keep going, it shows promise."

Flowery and graphic. What was that supposed to mean? I could change it, couldn't I? I felt as if I was being politely patted on the head and told to go back to my colouring books.

"Sorry if he's been blunt," said Jo.

"Oh, no, it's fine," I lied, forcing a smile. "I knew it was a long shot."

There was an awkward pause.

"Sam's got some news, too," chipped in Liam. "He's a psycho-criminal maaaaadman!"

"Eh?" laughed Jo.

I wanted to forget about it, at least for now, so in telling Jo the details I emphasized how I was now thinking Liam was right, and that there may have been less to the whole thing than I'd assumed.

Jo's response was disconcerting. "What sort of dog was it?" she said. She was being serious.

"I don't know," I said. "It was quite big, but it wasn't an Irish Wolfhound, or anything like that. It wasn't a Golden Retriever, I know what they look like. I don't really know about dogs. Why?"

"Just a coincidence." Jo shrugged. "At dinner last night, my dad was telling me about the running order of stories in his paper for this week. Third is a thing about pet snatchers. There've been several thefts in Hadlington and in the villages along the river."

"Does your dad always run the *Hadlington Courier*'s editorial decisions past you?" said Liam.

"No, of course not. He was telling me because the lead today is about a girl I used to be at playgroup with. I think he was a bit shocked. My mum was shocked, anyway."

"Shocked by what?" I said.

"This girl, Kat Brennan, has run away. She's the second from Elton Gardens to do that in less than a month. The police don't think there's any link, but Dad says they both had boyfriends in gangs."

"There you go," said Liam, pointing a finger at me. "Gangs again, Elton Gardens again."

"By the way," said Jo, "Dad also said the cops have confirmed that the dead guy in the park had an Elton Gardens address."

"Yeah, yeah, OK," I said. "When did this girl go missing?"

"Oh, last weekend sometime," said Jo.

"Not yesterday?" I said.

A scream in the night.

"No."

"But your mum was shocked."

"Well, yes," said Jo, "because we know her. Or knew her, years ago. I can barely remember her myself, but Mum kept shaking her head last night and saying what a nice family the Brennans were and how could Kat have got herself into trouble like that. Mum stuff."

I just couldn't help instantly leaping to conclusions. The dog I'd seen – it had to be one of the stolen ones! The scream I'd heard – it had to be the missing girl!

I felt like smacking my head against a brick wall. *Don't be a dribbling idiot*, I told myself. *Cut out the junior detective shit, life is not a paperback mystery plot!* At least I had the presence of mind not to say any of it out loud to Liam or Jo.

I wondered if I was overcompensating, because of the let-down over my article. I was looking for a story, a narrative that might be spun into a piece that *would* impress. Was I seeing connections that weren't there and coincidences that didn't exist, all for the sake of my ambitions? The thought made me feel even worse.

I managed to force everything to the back of my mind until the end-of-school bell went. School was harder work than I was used to. You could see why Maybrick High was so far up the league tables.

In the steady rush towards the main road, I found myself a couple of metres away from Emma Greenhill. She was chattering away with a girl from my class.

I wanted to talk to her, if only to help clarify some of my own thoughts. Speeding up a little, I managed to get ahead of them. Emma's friend said her goodbyes and walked over to a waiting car. Timing it just right, I accidentally-on-purpose nearly collided with Emma's school bag.

"Hello, Sam Hunter," she said cheerily, beaming at me. "How are you?"

"I'm, er, I'm fine," I said, desperately trying to

think of something to say. "I met your mum earlier."

"Did you? Oh, yes, she said she might go over and say hello. Isn't that weird, you're our new neighbours! I didn't know until this morning. Shall we walk home together?"

"Sure."

My conversation had dried up. Luckily, Emma was keen to have a moan about her physics class. I kept glancing at her profile as she spoke. How many glances would add up to a stare?

"Do you mind if I ask you something?" I said, once her physics class had been firmly put in its place.

"Uh-oh!" she giggled.

"Do you have a dog?"

"A dog?" she said. "No. Why?"

"I just wondered."

"I've never wanted pets, to be honest," she said. "My parents won't have dogs in the house, anyway. Did you know they carry lots of diseases? People don't generally know that. Mum told me she's had a couple of patients who died from things they caught off their dog. Cats are bad, too."

"No, I've never had a pet, either. We, er, never had room. Before."

"Where have you moved here from?" she said. The warmth of her voice made me feel as if I was the only living soul in her world.

"Oh, miles away," I said. "Near Birmingham. Er, can I ask you something else?"

"Uh-oh again."

"This might sound like a funny question."

"Like 'what colour is a kilo of noise'? That's a funny question."

I laughed. "No, like 'do you have an elderly relative staying in your house?'"

"An elderly relative?" she repeated, turning her blue-grey eyes on me. "What makes you ask that?"

"Oh, er, just something someone said."

"My grandpop lives with us."

"Nobody else? Your grandmother?"

It was her turn to laugh now. "My last grandmother died, er, thirty years ago. My oldest relative after Grandpop would be my Auntie Cass, and she lives in London. And she's not old, as such. Of course, my mother's way past forty, so she's pretty old. But whatever you do, don't say that to her, because she'll sulk. Seriously. And Grandpop never likes to be reminded of his age either. Hah! Speak of the devil!"

She waved at a man standing out on Maybrick Road. He raised his walking stick to her.

Emma's words made me feel… What? Confused? Intrigued? I wanted to believe the best of her, I really did. She was either a truly brilliant liar, or she really *didn't* have any pets or elderly relatives. Which supported the idea of the face as a fear-fuelled illusion, but put the rest of the day's thoughts and theories back to square one.

She had to be covering up about the dog, just like her mother. She just had to be. I suppose I was being pathetically naïve, but I simply couldn't reconcile this funny, beautiful girl with today's theories and discussions about the previous night.

It actually went through my mind that perhaps I should keep that appointment at her mother's surgery after all. For a few moments, I genuinely wondered if I was in need of help and advice. That's how quickly and easily the Emma Greenhill effect had entered my bloodstream.

Emma hurried forward and flung her arms around the man. "What are you doing here, Pops? Are you spying on me?"

"I was out for a walk, my love, when I saw all

these youngsters coming out of school. I thought I might as well stop and wait for you."

He was wiry and upright, ex-military if his regimented body language was anything to go by. He was wrapped in a camel hair coat, with a striped scarf tucked neatly round his neck. His shoes were polished to a shine, and the walking stick seemed to be an affectation, since he clearly didn't need to lean on it. His face was wrinkled and rough, but his eyes were bright and glittering. The sprightliest pensioner I'd ever seen. His white hair was slicked back, in a 1950s style. He certainly bore no resemblance to the macabre, cadaverous thing at the window.

"Pops, this is my new friend Sam Hunter. Sam, this is my grandfather."

'My new friend' she called me! My heart raced.

Something in the man's tone told me that he knew perfectly well who I was. "So you're one of the new people at number three, are you?" His voice was snappy and commanding, the no-nonsense voice of someone used to hearing the word 'yes' a lot. "Pleasure to meet you, lad."

"Thank you. I've now met most of my new neighbours."

"Indeed," he said.

"We can all walk home together," said Emma.

"I think Sam has an appointment, don't you, Sam?" said her grandad.

My mind did a kind of double take.

Emma looked at me. They were both looking at me, kindly but expectant. Insistent.

"I didn't realize, Sam," said Emma. "Sorry, you go ahead."

She knew what appointment he meant. She didn't have to ask. A twist of nerves tightened in my gut.

"I, er…" I stumbled. "I'll have to give it a miss, I'm afraid. I've got lots of homework."

The old man's glittering eyes took me apart piece by piece, but his expression was carefully benevolent, a hard mask of sympathy and understanding that pulled the twist inside me even tighter.

"Oh. Now, that's disappointing." His words were heavy with disapproval, a passive-aggressive gentility that made me want to leap to attention, to apologize unreservedly, to rush to where I was supposed to be.

"Another time," I said hurriedly.

"I'm sure you'll feel better for a chat," he said.

"No?"

"Sorry," I mumbled.

"Oh dear," he said amiably, "my daughter-in-law will have gone to some trouble to clear her schedule, but not to worry, of course. Your choice."

"I'll see you tomorrow, Sam," said Emma brightly, shining her smile on me.

"Yes," I said.

I rushed away. It might be more accurate to say I fled.

The events of the previous night had given me cause to believe that the Greenhills weren't quite as squeaky clean as their reputation suggested, that they were harbouring some sort of secret.

On top of that, I now had to add a second suspicion: that there was some kind of ulterior motive for my appointment with Emma's mother. It wasn't neighbourliness on the part of Dr Greenhill, it wasn't the kindly attentions of a hard-working GP.

There was something more to it. Why else would both Emma and her grandfather even be aware of it? What this ulterior motive could possibly be, I hadn't the faintest idea. All I knew was that by avoiding the appointment, I was clearly causing annoyance.

If I hadn't left my room the previous night, then I might not even have noticed the Greenhills' strangely unified front on the subject of the surgery. However, with seeds of suspicion already sown in my mind, this new development made those seeds sprout and flourish. I couldn't for one minute imagine what connection there might be between my experience the previous night and Caroline Greenhill's appointment book, but I was in no doubt whatsoever that a connection was there. I just had to find it.

I have to confess, in seeking answers I was at least partly motivated by selfishness, by a desire to write something that Jo's dad would accept. I wanted to bring in a story, plain and simple. A good one. I wanted to get ahead, as my parents had never managed to do. I wanted to prove, to myself and to the *Hadlington Courier*, that I *could* be a serious journalist, and that I wasn't playing around. I suppose, looking back, I had what my mum would have called a chip on my shoulder.

About three hours later, when Mum, Dad and I were having our tea around the table in the dining room,

I discovered that both Mum and Dad had kept their appointments with Dr Greenhill, earlier in the day. I looked back and forth between them, resting my knife and fork on my plate.

"And what happened?" I said.

"At the surgery?" said Dad, cutting up a roast potato. "Nothing. What d'you mean?"

"What did Dr Greenhill do?"

"Do?" he said. "Nothing. We chatted."

"About what?"

"It's private," said Mum. "Patient confidentiality."

"About what?" I insisted.

Dad shrugged. "General health stuff. My medical history. A chat."

"Did she examine you?" I said. "Prescribe you anything?"

"Don't be nosy," said Dad.

"Did she?"

"Don't be nosy, Sam," said Mum.

Dad chuckled. "She really is a striking woman, that Caroline Greenhill."

Mum tutted gently and shook her head. "Haven't the fitters done a good job on the carpets." She rubbed her socks against the freshly laid floor.

I was so wrapped up in my own concerns that it didn't register with me at the time, not properly, but both of them seemed in a slightly odd mood. Slightly fuzzy, as if they'd had a few drinks, yet fully alert. It's hard to describe. It seemed as if their thoughts were always on something else, somewhere else, as if they were wrapped up in an inner problem that needed immense thought.

If only I'd taken more notice of it, there and then.

"I tell you what," said Dad, "It's nice to find a GP who takes the time to do regular check-ups for her patients."

"It is." Mum nodded.

"What do you need regular check-ups for?" I exclaimed.

"It's recommended," said Mum, as if I was asking a stupid question.

"Who by?" I said.

"We're not getting any younger, you know," said Dad. "It's time we looked after ourselves."

"You're only just over fifty," I said. "You're not exactly senile."

"I saw Mrs Gifford earlier," said Mum. "They have check-ups with Doctor Greenhill, too, and so do the

Daltons. How are you getting on with Emma?"

"Emma?" I blinked. "Fine."

That shut me up.

"That's nice," said Mum. "I hear she's a lovely girl."

Days went by in a blur. I really was very busy
with homework. There was more to catch up on
than Liam had estimated. Most of it was relatively
straightforward, but some of the science and maths
were brain-numbing.

Nothing out of the ordinary happened for a
while. Because there were no further developments,
and nothing more I could add to the news report I
was compiling in my head, my nervousness abated
slightly, as nerves usually do.

My uneasiness about the Greenhills began to slip
to the back of my mind, just a little. I think what
encouraged my gradual change of heart was that
Emma was just so ... well, normal.

I stayed friendly with her. Perhaps I should say
she stayed friendly with me. We talked about this
and that, as if nothing had happened and nothing
unusual was ever likely to happen, but I didn't go

out of my way to be part of her circle, or anything like that. I have to admit, if I'm being honest, I was pleased – no, not pleased: delighted, and flattered – that her popularity reflected back on me, so that many more people started to say 'hi' to the new kid.

Recording it all now, I feel ashamed for falling in line like that, but being accepted and liked by my peers had a powerful pull. I was drawn to Emma, there's no denying it.

I did try to act casual with her, even uninterested, because I still didn't know what to make of her. On the one hand, she never wavered from being the most-admired girl in our year group, if not the whole school. She was her regular, lively, very-easy-to-like self. On the other hand, my doubts and strange misgivings about her family continued to circle in the background, like a shark waiting to strike.

I spent a lot of time with Emma in the couple of weeks before half term. It was purely by chance that the two of us were assigned to the same coursework project in English: assembling a website containing full details on a local issue or event.

Thinking about it now, it's not beyond the realms of possibility that Emma, or her family, pulled the odd string and had us put together deliberately. In order for her to keep an eye on me, I mean, to make sure that I wasn't doing anything they might not like. I've no evidence for it, just the vaguest impression. When we found out what the coursework would entail, before we were split into workgroups, I happened to mention to Emma that I was keen on a career in investigative journalism. I only said it off the top of my head, in passing, but I said it because – again, I'm ashamed to admit – I wanted her to like me. Maybe even admire me.

"Yeah?" she said, smiling. I took the cheery expression on her face to be approval but, thinking back, it might have been something else. It might have been masking her real reaction.

I prefer to believe that our team-up for the assignment was simply one of those things. But you never know.

"You jammy sod," said Liam with a grin, when the coursework lists were posted up in our classroom. "She's not even in our tutor group!"

"Dirty job, but someone's gotta do it," I smiled. "At least you're with Jo, and not lumbered with some useless hanger-on. She's not in our tutor group either."

"Ah, bless our school's inclusive cross-curricular policies," grinned Liam. I don't think he meant to show how pleased he was. I never did get to the bottom of his reluctance to tell Jo how he felt about her.

Emma suggested, sensibly, that our project cover the reopening of the Hadlington public library, partly because it was a ready-made story that perfectly fitted the bill, but mostly because her family's involvement in the whole thing gave us quick access to useful stuff. Detailed plans of the library building, past and present, for example, and an interview with the guy in charge of the refurbishments.

The Greenhills had personally donated a large sum to the town authorities, in order to prevent the library from closing. Its interior was being completely redesigned and refitted by firms whose bosses were personal friends of the family. Five years earlier, they'd funded a nearby centre for drug-addiction treatment, under similar circumstances.

Our project went well. Emma and I assembled our material with efficiency, and we collaborated on constructing the website, me on overall construction (with some input from Liam), she on design and navigation.

I need to record the details of one particular conversation we had. It didn't really strike me as anything odd or unexpected at the time, but it has a direct bearing on what I discovered later. It's not that she let anything slip exactly, it's that she revealed things that became relevant to my later understanding of the Greenhills, and their true nature. It marked a small change in how I felt about her.

We were close to finishing the project. It was a Thursday, and the completed thing had to be in on Monday morning. We were in what the school pretentiously calls the learning resources room, sitting on armless foam lounging chairs, with school laptops on our knees. Kids padded around the bookshelves that stood in long rows before us, and a teacher marked homework behind the curved information desk nearby.

"Have you got the photo from last week's *Courier*?" I asked.

"Oh, yes, sorry, I'll drop it into the shared folder now," said Emma. I found it and slotted it into place on the relevant page. There was her mum at the reopening ceremony, shaking hands with the mayor and the leaders of the town council.

Neither of us said anything for a minute or two. We each stared at our screens and tapped our keyboards.

Finally, Emma puffed out her cheeks. "Are you bored?" she whispered. "I'm getting bored with this."

"There's still plenty to do," I said. "I'm happy to leave it for now, but we won't have time tomorrow."

"Oh bugger, yeah," she sighed. "It's that stupid careers thing all day. Forgot about that."

"If you like, I could come over at the weekend. I mean, you only live a few hundred metres away!" Strange as it might sound, there really wasn't any agenda behind what I said. I didn't for a second think it might be a chance to make a move on her, or anything like that, and I certainly didn't feel any of the burning urgency to see inside the Priory that was to consume me not long afterwards.

I would have asked her over to ours, but the thought of my mother going all gooey over her was too terrible to even contemplate. Emma would leave our house with the unambiguous impression that my parents thought of her as a lovely girl and ideal girlfriend material. Which, of course, they did.

She smiled at me. "No, you're right, we should

finish now." Something must have flashed across my face, because she added: "Sorry, I'm not being funny, it's just that I very rarely have anyone over to my house."

"Really? Why's that?"

She looked a little sheepish. "Well, I know it sounds silly, but I tend to guard my own personal space. If you see what I mean. I like to have lots of friends, as you know, and I like to be doing things and going places, but I also like to keep something that's just for me. I keep my own home private. Sorry, I know that sounds weird."

"No, not at all," I said. It did sound slightly odd, but no more than that. "I try to keep my parents out of my room all the time! The notice on my door saying 'sod off' doesn't seem to work, though."

She laughed. "Mum and Dad think I'm peculiar. They have their cronies and business types over for dinner all the time."

I looked back at the screen in front of me. "It must be strange, seeing your mum in the paper like that."

Emma shrugged. "It happens now and again. You'd be surprised how blasé you get about it! Mum and Dad are always being papped at charity dos –

they love it. No, really, they do. They like to be seen to be doing their bit for the plebs."

I blinked. Had I heard that right? "Sorry?"

"Oh, you know what I mean," she said.

"Plebs?" I said, with exaggerated emphasis.

"Oh, stop it," she smiled. "You know what I mean. Charity work. There's nothing wrong with that."

"I agree."

"They collected the money to set up a new food bank last Christmas. Sometimes, you have to step in and do things for people that they won't do for themselves."

I kept my tone deliberately jokey. "I thiiiink it's more a question of *can't* than *won't*. I'm pretty sure users of food banks aren't just too lazy to go to Tesco. Hmm, can't say I had you down as a closet snob."

"I am *not* a snob," she laughed, wide-eyed. Her mouth wrinkled into a semi-grin. "It's just that … y'know, there are some people … to whom I *am* superior." She giggled. She was making a joke of it, but she said it with such ease that I felt I was glimpsing an aspect of her I'd never seen before.

Even so, it didn't ring any particular alarm

bells. It should have done, but it didn't. Although it marked the first time I'd ever seen her as having 'Hadlingtonist' attitudes, I think I might still have forgiven her anything at that point.

Maybrick was full of snobs, I reasoned logically. Some of it was bound to rub off on her. She came from a wealthy family, so a little right-wing grit, a little detachment from certain realities, was simply a product of her sheltered upbringing and her privileged surroundings. No more than that.

I reasoned it away, but my heart took a step back from her. The first of many.

We brushed the subject aside and returned to our project. It took a while to finish, but we did it in the end. We got good marks for it, too.

Meanwhile, in the run-up to half term, I never so much as caught sight of her grandfather or her mother. Messages were relayed to me that my original appointment at Caroline Greenhill's surgery had been rearranged, twice. Still wary, I missed both of them. In the continued absence of any clue as to why the Greenhills were so keen to get me there, continuing to keep my distance seemed the best policy. I missed both rescheduled appointments, but nothing happened. Dr Greenhill appeared to give up asking after that.

I still hadn't had so much as a glimpse of Emma's dad, Byron Greenhill, either. Sometimes, that Renault people carrier would be in the drive of Bierce Priory, and sometimes another car, a red sports model that I assumed to be his. I heard he spent a lot of time working away, or abroad.

There was nothing more in the papers about runaways or missing pets. The *Hadlington Courier* had a few slow-news weeks.

It was what happened with Mum and Dad that cranked up my suspicions again. No – more than that. Mum and Dad were the tipping point.

It was little things, at first. Dad stopped doing all the small DIY jobs around the house, and Mum stopped nagging him about them. The normal pattern of behaviour in our house was for Mum to identify something that needed doing, then she'd nag Dad to do it, then she'd nag him again, then he'd tell her to do it herself if it was so bloody important, then she'd say that she damn well would if she had the time, then he'd finally get it done. This fixed, unchanging pattern had been completely cast aside.

It wasn't anything to do with the fact that we had money now, that we could afford to have someone else do these things. They just left them undone, as if they neither of them could be bothered. A couple of the bannisters on the stairs had been knocked out of alignment when we moved in, when the removal people were lugging stuff upstairs. I asked Mum why they were left sticking out like that. She just shrugged and said, "Does it matter?"

Dad started composing songs again, which was something he hadn't done in years, not properly. At first, I was delighted, for him and for Mum. I hoped it might signify a whole new lease of life for him. It seemed that by finally having commercial success, he'd found a fresh creativity. But what he played us on one of his guitars was terrible, nothing like the material he'd done in the past. Overlong, dreary, almost tuneless. Mum clapped and laughed. I just smiled and nodded, wondering what on earth he was doing. At the same time, he stopped adding to his collection of so-called memorabilia, despite for the first time having more than enough cash to indulge his habit.

On top of all that, Mum eased up on the work

hours. Having her at home more was nice, but she also eased up on things like showering and putting petrol in the car. She was a good cook, much better than Dad, but her repertoire gradually shrank to three or four dishes, which she repeated day after day. When I tentatively asked her why, she seemed puzzled by the question, and told me if I didn't like it then I knew where the kitchen was, you cheeky little sod.

Both of them were changing. Slowly, subtly, but definitely. And not for the better.

That slight oddity in their mood, the one I'd noticed before, was set in now. It was their normal state. I'm not sure if anyone who didn't know them well, or at least fairly well, would have noticed much difference but to me, living with them, they'd become … the word that comes to mind is detached.

Finally, one evening, the reason suddenly hit me, because of something specific I noticed.

We were in the living room. I was reading and they were flopped on the (new) sofa, Mum ordering the groceries delivery on the laptop, Dad chuckling at *EastEnders*. When the truth dawned on me, it felt like running into a brick wall.

The changes in their behaviour had reminded me of some aspects of what we'd been told to look out for in our friends, when they did the warning-us-off-drugs thing at school. I didn't for one second think that Mum and Dad were getting hold of anything illegal. Dad had always steered well clear of anything like that, despite his music business connections. He'd had a friend who'd overdosed when he was still in his teens, and it had put him off for life.

And they weren't drinking. They'd never really been drinkers. There were some beers and a bottle of wine in the fridge, but that was about it. Where was this peculiar dopiness coming from?

The icy sensation washed over me as several thoughts clicked into place, one after the other:

They seemed permanently laid-back, permanently pleased and smiley. Just like the Giffords next door. And the Daltons.

What did Mum and Dad, and the Giffords and the Daltons have in common?

Dr Greenhill's GP surgery. Their pointless check-ups, as far as Mum and Dad were concerned at least. Neither of my parents were exactly in poor health. The Giffords, being that much older, I could understand, but not the Daltons, or us Hunters.

Dr Greenhill was…?

Supplying them all with something? Tranquillizers, antidepressants? Something else?

There and then, I asked Mum and Dad about it, as subtly as I could. They flatly denied there was any kind of medication in the house, beyond a box of paracetamol in the kitchen drawer.

Were they lying to me? Were they even *aware* that they were lying to me?

Any why? For God's sake, why?

I almost dismissed the whole thing as beyond belief. What possible reason could our GP – any GP – have for dosing up a whole street? But, again and again, my mind kept snapping back to Emma's mum, and Emma, and her grandad, all taking for granted that I was going to comply with the check-up thing. "I'm sure you'll feel better for a chat," Emma's grandad had said.

The more it churned around inside me, the creepier it got.

And what was it old Mr Gifford had said on the day after we moved in? About Emma's dad? The ex-surgeon. One of the country's leading psychopharmacologists. And what do psychopharmacologists do? I looked it up immediately. They create drugs. Ones that affect mood, and thinking, and behaviour. Some of the things that had been developed over the years were terrifying.

These thoughts and connections spiralled through my head because of that specific thing I noticed: I could see tiny, thin lines on Mum and Dad's upper lips. Had they not been there before? Had they only just appeared? Had I been missing them for days? I didn't know. Mum and Dad now had the same barely-there, slightly yellow runny noses that all the neighbours had when we met them for the first time.

Correction, that the neighbours *still* had, because I'd seen Mr Dalton ferrying Greye to his playgroup only the day before, and I'd talked to Mrs Gifford as she'd tidied her front garden at the weekend. I'd seen them dab the same little trails from their noses as they'd done weeks earlier. And I'd thought to myself that, yuck, that virus was hanging around for a long time.

My parents and the neighbours showed the same

behaviour. And had apparently caught the same tenacious virus. Which I miraculously hadn't. The only difference was that I'd never been for a check-up with Dr Greenhill, and they all went regularly.

There seemed to be only one logical conclusion. Something was being done to them.

Chapter Six

I had no proof. Coincidences and suspicions weren't proof. The utter absurdity of my so-called logical conclusion kept hammering away at my brain, throwing out questions, until I just couldn't hold it all in my head at once.

After all the wavering, and the indecision, and the puzzling, I decided to do some research on the Greenhills. I'd caught the scent of the story I'd been after, it's true, but more than anything else I wanted to investigate for my own peace of mind.

I hoped I was wrong – I want to make that clear. I didn't want to discover that my parents, or anyone else, really were being doped up by Caroline Greenhill. It seemed both horrific and ridiculous.

More than once, it has crossed my mind that it might have been easier to give in, avoid any emotional pain and go for those check-ups myself.

I could have let myself get with the programme, and remained in blissful ignorance.

But I needed to find the truth. If these new fears were true, how did this connect to what I'd witnessed that night? Had someone, perhaps, been testing medication on that dog? Could it be that it wasn't injured, but doped? Had the scream been one of discovery after all? Had Emma – or someone – walked in on the experiment? And if there was some sort of experimentation involved, were there now any reasons to connect the Greenhills to the murder in the park? Could the victim have been part of some sort of experiment himself, as I'd originally thought? Had I been too quick to believe the prevailing view about the killing? If so, why had that particular man died, and not some other?

What my research would actually accomplish, I didn't stop to consider. Beyond the self-centred chance to write it all up for the *Courier*, that is.

Half term started on 18th October. Once school work was out of the way, I'd have the best part of a week to dig up whatever I could. As we left school on that Friday, I let Liam and Jo in on my plans. I mentioned my suspicions of doping, and my reasons for them, but I also laid it on so thick that even I baulked at the idea. Nevertheless, we had a long conversation in which they flipped from alarm, to derision, and back again.

"Wouldn't it be easier to just become Emma's boyfriend and ask?" said Liam. "I think she likes you."

"She doesn't have boyfriends, remember," said Jo.

"OK, close friend, then. Get yourself invited over to her house."

"She doesn't do that either," I said.

"That's true," said Jo. "I don't know anyone who's seen inside her house."

"I want to keep my distance, anyway," I said.

"I think Sam's right," said Jo.

"About the Greenhills?" said Liam. "Don't be daft."

"I meant about keeping his distance," said Jo. She gave me a look that I couldn't quite interpret. "I'm keeping an open mind about the Greenhills. If you unearth anything scandalous, can my dad have the exclusive?"

"Absolutely," I said.

"I assume you're going to be too busy to come over and help me build a new computer then?" said Liam.

"Text me in a few days," I said.

By Monday, I'd begun work. From my room, I combed through every publicly accessible database I could find. I paid for temporary membership of various online academic and news media archives, and got Liam to hack me into a couple more I needed to be an employee to use. I sifted through information at the upgraded Hadlington public library and the County Records Office, and found half a dozen slim volumes on the history of the town and the surrounding areas.

I even managed to contact the author of one of those volumes by email, and asked her a few questions based on what she'd mentioned about Bierce Priory in her book. To my surprise, she'd worked alongside Ken Greenhill, Emma's grandfather, at the town council and had known the Greenhill family in years gone by. Off the record, she repeated a number of items of minor tittle-tattle about them, and in particular about Ken Greenhill.

In just a few days, I'd managed to piece together a reasonably detailed picture. The thing about being The Country's Leading Whatever is that a lot of other people know who you are. The same goes if you're someone who used to appear on TV, no matter how long ago. Or if you used to be a leading light in local politics. Between them, Byron, Caroline and Ken Greenhill had notched up hundreds of mentions in local and overseas newspapers, official documents, academic and medical journals, scientific blogs, political diaries and expert testimonies, plus a smattering of interviews and entries in various high-society calendars, even a few appearances in gossip columns.

Assembled from many sources, my research into the Greenhills could be summarized like this:

Emma's parents, Byron and Caroline, were both born in 1972 and met as undergraduates at Oxford University. Caroline's family were very wealthy, one step away from aristocracy, but by the time she married Byron in 1993 her only surviving relative was her elder brother Vincent, who is now a parliamentary undersecretary in the Home Office.

Byron's father, Ken Greenhill, was originally called Kurt Hugelgrun. The Hugelgruns were a dynasty of industrialists from Austria. (Many of these details came from a German public archive, which

Jo managed to translate bits of for me – she was taking German at school.) The Hugelgrun fortune was created by two things: munitions manufacture for the German army during World War I, and a patented medicine produced by a pharmaceutical company they owned, which was used extensively during the flu pandemic of 1918-19, an outbreak that killed well over fifty million people.

The Hugelgruns kept out of politics, playing no part in the formation of the Third Reich or the horrors that followed. However, they left Austria in 1938, eleven months before the outbreak of World War II. Upon their arrival in Britain, official records list them as being refugees from the Nazis, escaping persecution. However, there was no record of them doing anything in Austria that could have got them persecuted. Their reason for leaving the country might have centred around a series of murders that took place in the suburbs of Vienna in the mid 30s. Over a period of two and a half years, the bodies of seven women and three men were found dumped in the city's narrow, twisting alleyways. All had been sliced open with surgical precision, and internal organs removed, including eyes, brains and lungs.

Comparisons were inevitably drawn with the Ripper murders in Whitechapel in 1888.

Suspicion fell on Gottfried Hugelgrun, Ken/Kurt's father. Three of the victims had worked for Hugelgrun companies and Gottfried, then aged thirty-six, had twice been seen by other employees at locations that tied in with crime scenes. Gottfried was a biochemist, but was known to have an extensive laboratory at his home, where numerous preserved organs – human and animal – were openly on display for guests. There was no actual evidence to link him to any of the killings so charges were never brought.

Nothing relating to these murders appears in any UK information source, and there are no mentions of them in any true crime books I've been able to find. This is probably because the original investigation appears to have been patchy, and there's very little documentation beyond the initial autopsy reports.

Gottfried sold up and arrived in England with his wife, Marta, his mother, Helga, and his infant son, Kurt. Almost the first thing he did was to become a British citizen, translating his name from German to become Godfrey Greenhill, his son becoming Kenneth, his wife becoming Martha. Some mystery surrounds the fate of Helga. She vanishes from official county records during World War II, and it's not known how she died. Ken was only four years old when the family left Austria, and claimed in later years to have no recollection of his original home. Gottfried bought Bierce Priory less than a month after landing at Dover.

The house was built in 1812, on what was then open land. The area where Priory Mews was added in the 1920s was originally stables. There exist several poorly preserved photographs of liveried footmen standing beside the low, shed–like stable buildings. It seems that a great deal of work was done to Bierce Priory at the same time as the three Priory Mews houses were being constructed, but what exactly was done is not recorded, beyond the addition of that annexe to the side of the main structure.

In the late 1940s Gottfried, like his mother, vanishes from official records. Ken Greenhill went to a private school in Surrey, then to Cambridge University, and volunteered for army duty rather than being called up for National Service. He left the army with the rank of lieutenant in 1958 and went straight into local politics.

Ken Greenhill spent his entire career at Hadlington's council offices, in one capacity or another, retiring in 1995. Among many other things, he was responsible for a number of housing developments, including Elton Gardens. Newspaper pictures from 1963 show him shaking hands with the chairman of a large building company. He also had the path behind Priory Mews laid, the one leading down to the river, and he set the catchment areas of all the local schools. Given the frequency with which he was applauded for one municipal project after another, he must have built up an enormous network of influential contacts, as well as having the trust and support of the town's population. It seems he was a demanding person to work for, and caused controversy several times by sacking council staff whom he deemed to be not pulling their weight.

Ken married a woman called Vivienne Hobcourt in 1971. Like Ken's eventual daughter-in-law Caroline, Vivienne came from a well-connected family, the heirs to a large fortune made in South African diamond mining. They had two sons, Byron and Leonard. The younger brother is now chief constable of the county's police, a man highly respected for taking a tough stance on crime (although why Elton Gardens apparently remains a permanent trouble spot is a mystery). Vivienne is said to have run away in 1975, abandoning her sons, although where she went, and why, is unknown. The incident caused local tongues to wag, but public sympathies were totally on Ken's side.

Byron Greenhill has had an even more glittering career than either his brother or father, winning a number of international prizes and serving on three government committees relating to medical issues. His research work has been mainly in the field of developing medicines for use in psychiatric wards, for calming and controlling dangerous and disturbed patients.

Between 1988 and 1993, when Byron was in his teens and early twenties, a string of murders and other serious crimes took place in and around Hadlington, which caused a brief but intense flurry of interest in the national media. Seven corpses were found, dissected and dumped. Organs and other body parts went missing from Hadlington's nearest hospital. A doctor at the hospital was found stabbed to death. It was thought he stumbled upon one of the organ thefts taking place, and was subjected to what the press called 'a frenzied attack with a knife and a pair of scissors'. The police officer leading the investigation, Detective Inspector Jeffrey Coombs, received a commendation for tracking down and arresting a homeless alcoholic called Albert Small, who was sentenced to life imprisonment and then killed in Pentonville by another prisoner in 1996. Small's defence lawyer had argued that his client had an unshakable alibi for two of the deaths, and showed that the man's health prevented him from having the physical strength necessary to commit the crimes.

Nothing whatsoever links Byron, or any of the Greenhills, to these crimes, apart from the coincidence that Detective Inspector Coombs was a close friend of Ken Greenhill. However, Byron was involved in an incident reported as a brief 'late news' item in the *Hadlington Courier* in March 1993, which then received no further coverage at all. He was arrested by police after a woman, walking alone through the park, claimed she was grabbed from behind and threatened with a knife. That single, short news report is the only evidence that the incident ever took place. Byron's accuser was committed to a psychiatric unit in January 1994.

Caroline Greenhill made a similarly brief appearance in a national tabloid's salacious rumours column in 2007, although her actual name wasn't printed. A two-paragraph boxed section beginning 'Which ex-TV doc and wife of a prominent scientist…' claimed she'd been questioned by police following 'an attempt to threaten' a senior officer. The man in question, who was two command ranks below Chief Inspector Leonard Greenhill, was reassigned to a neighbouring police force a few months later.

The only reports relating to Emma Greenhill I could find were notices in the *Courier* about her wins with the school badminton team, and her triumphs in the district Under-Sixteens music contest.

I compiled my dossier on the Greenhills with a growing sense of unease. There was more than I've summarized here. By cross-referencing facts about Byron Greenhill's work – mainly comments in medical journals about where in the world he was conducting research – it was possible to correlate extended times he spent in both Chicago and Berlin with reports of 'dissection' murders carried out in those cities.

There was nothing concrete to go on, nothing definite and proven, but I was rapidly getting the creeping sensation that the Greenhills were hiding something truly horrible. Taking everything into consideration, I thought that the most probable scenario was that there was simply a streak of insanity in the family. Byron seemed the likeliest current candidate, because of those overseas correlations. Did he have periods of insanity? Did he battle severe psychosis? Had he murdered the man in the park, and attacked that dog I'd seen? Had members of earlier generations suffered from the same forms of illness?

Might that be the true explanation for the face I'd seen at the window? The unnatural expression, the staring eyes?

Could that be what drove Byron's research? Was he trying to cure himself? Were the other Greenhills desperately trying to keep his secret, and hush it all up?

At the end of the half-term week, I slapped the laptop shut and buried my face in my hands. I was beginning to think that the only insane person was me.

Downstairs, in the living room, that week's edition of the *Hadlington Courier* reported another dead body found on the banks of the Arvan, this time well out of town, about ten miles upstream. Its hands and feet had been removed.

"At least that one's got nothing to do with Elton Gardens," said Dad, flicking over to the Property section. "Crikey, there's one for sale at the end of Maybrick Road for nearly three million."

I was watching my parents closely now. They remained 'adjusted', perfectly contented in themselves, but speculation about what might be coursing through their veins kept me wary and on edge, and more determined than ever to uncover some hard evidence.

On the local TV news that teatime, the parents of the second missing girl, Kat Brennan, the one Jo used to know, made a tearful appeal for Kat to get in touch with them. The girl's mother, barely able to look at the camera, begged her daughter to come home. It didn't matter what she'd done, she sobbed, they just wanted her home safe. It was heartbreaking. And, once again, I couldn't help but leap to a troubling conclusion.

A photo of Kat stayed on screen, as a reporter interviewed Chief Inspector Leonard Greenhill. His officers were actively pursuing several lines of enquiry, he said, but as Elton Gardens was a notorious area for gang activity, he felt that there were grounds to fear the worst. No, it had not been his idea to hold this press conference here today. Yes, he would appeal to any member of the public to come forward if they were able to provide any further information relevant to the case.

I called Jo, and arranged to meet her dad at the *Hadlington Courier* the following morning.

The offices were located in the middle of the town centre, two upper floors of a small building that also housed a row of shops and a dentist's practice. The weekly paper was only sparsely staffed on a Saturday, but it was easy to imagine the place alive with activity. Desks were close together and surrounded by filing cabinets. Papers were piled up on almost every surface.

Jo's dad, Martin, was a plump man with thick glasses and neatly parted hair that was going grey in a ragged band around the edges. His crisp white shirt was rapidly coming untucked from the front of his trousers. He showed me into a small section of the office that was partitioned off, and wheeled a squeaky swivel chair out for me to sit on. He plonked himself down behind his desk.

"It's nice to finally meet you, Sam," he said.

"Yes," I said, suddenly conscious that I might be in a job-interview situation. "Jo, umm, mentioned that I might be able to do some work experience here. Maybe after the spring term?"

Martin sniffed and nodded a couple of times. "Yes, I'm sure we can sort something out. It's good to find someone your age who's keen. It's a dying trade, I'm afraid. Local papers will be all but gone in a few years." He held out both palms. "Don't want to put you off!"

"You won't," I grinned.

"OK, Jo said you had something for me, that might be a bit … iffy?"

I opened the lever arch file I'd brought with me. Suddenly, I felt very foolish. In the file were over a hundred pages of text and photos I'd printed at home, and sitting there in that office they suddenly seemed to amount to nonsense.

"Er, well," I said. "It's more that I'd like your

opinion. What I've got here is... Well, I hope... Perhaps I should just start with what's happened since I moved to Hadlington?"

He sat back a little. "Off you go, I'm all ears."

With nerves biting at my stomach, I outlined what I'd observed and experienced, and set out the research I'd done over the week. As I spoke, I removed pages from the file and placed them in front of him, pointing out things in photographs or old newspaper reports. He looked at them all carefully, peering beneath his glasses to examine one or two items more closely, and stacked them all neatly to one side of his desk.

When I'd finished, he sniffed again and took a final look through the pages. He leaned forward on his desk, rubbing his chin thoughtfully.

"OK," he said at last, "here's the good news. Young man, you have the makings of a first-class journalist, you really do. You've clearly got a nose for a story, and this research is better than most of the hacks in this place could turn in." He sat back and paused. He was choosing his words carefully. "The bad news is, there's nothing I can do with this, and you're almost certainly wrong."

129

"You think so?" I said. "I do actually want to be wrong, believe it or not."

"Look at it this way," he said, scratching his nose. "Which of these two scenarios is the more plausible? One, the Greenhills are drugging people, for purposes unknown. Or perhaps, going on the rest of what you've got here, in order to keep people docile in case they happen to spot funny goings-on at Bierce Priory. Goings-on, such as: the Greenhills might be involved in an assortment of very nasty crimes, which is possibly, according to your theory, to do with one or more of them suffering psychotic episodes. Yeah?"

I nodded cautiously.

"Scenario two. The Greenhills are well known, very respected, generous donors to charity, and so on and so on. The person raising questions about them is a lone teenager, and from the look of you a rather stressed-out one, at that. You're putting two and two together and making six and a half. Which of those two scenarios would *you* believe?"

"The second, obviously," I said glumly. "I do realize how weird it sounds. Do I really look stressed out?"

"You do," said Martin. "I'm guessing this has been preying on your mind? But cold viruses *can* hang around for months, these days, y'know? Look, the Greenhills are important people in Hadlington, but I'm not exactly their biggest fan. Ken Greenhill is an arrogant son of a bitch, frankly. I'd love to print something that'd take him down a peg or two, I really would. And Byron Greenhill makes a lot of people's flesh crawl. 'Self-basting' our editor here calls him. But what you've got here are suspicions and loose connections. You need hard proof. Catch Caroline Greenhill with a syringe in her hands. Photograph Byron running amok with a meat cleaver. Anything less is nothing at all. Do you see what I'm getting at?"

"Yes, I do."

"You might get one of the tabloids in London willing to run with something, but even then it's unlikely. And you know why? I'm not sure you've considered this angle yet."

I frowned. "Why?"

He sniffed. "Ninety per cent of the law in this country has got nothing to do with justice, young man. Remember that. It's about protection.

131

The protected survive, the unprotected fall. The Greenhills have a lot of influential friends, and they have enough money to pay for a whole army of lawyers. If you start throwing accusations at them, they're going to start throwing lawyers at you. Fact. And everyone at this paper, if we printed those accusations."

"You're right," I sighed, "I hadn't considered that."

"Those instances you mentioned, of stories appearing briefly? You can bet your life that the Greenhills got their legal Rottweilers to squash them. If there's no hard proof, it's all just opinion. You haven't put any of this stuff out online, have you?"

"No."

"Keep it that way, unless you want lawyers and a million online loonies howling at you."

I gathered up all my research, and clipped it back into the file. I felt like an idiot.

"Look, Sam," said Martin. "It's not even like I don't believe you. No, scratch that, I don't think you're right, not for a second – the implications are just beyond rational. But I'm willing to be proved wrong. OK? I'm willing to keep an open mind. Jesus, you've only got to look at the headlines from the past few years to see that the most astonishing cover-ups are possible. In politics, in the media, in the police, almost anywhere. And for every one that gets exposed, you can be sure there are a dozen others, maybe a hundred others. Money is power, and enough power means you can do whatever the hell you like, right or wrong, good or bad. The only rule people like that stick to is: don't get caught."

I clutched the file to my chest and stood up, the swivel chair squeaking loudly. "I'm sorry I've wasted your time."

Martin laughed. "You haven't. Honestly, Sam, you haven't. You could be really good at this job. When you want to arrange to come in for a week, give me a call."

"Really?"

"Yeah, really. OK?"

"Thanks," I said through a half-smile.

I walked home instead of taking the bus. I needed to think. Running through all the research in my head, and everything I'd seen for myself, the only thing that became clear was that no explanation I'd considered so far appeared to fit *all* the evidence. No, mustn't call it evidence. It wasn't evidence yet.

What could I do now? Should I wait, and hope that something more substantial would turn up? And what would that mean anyway? More deaths? How far did all this have to go before I could and should start blaming myself for not getting proper evidence sooner?

They had to have me marked down as a potential troublemaker, because of my refusal to go to Caroline Greenhill's surgery. They were probably keeping an equally close eye on me.

Did they know I'd just been to see Jo's dad?

No, probably not. The only people who knew I was going to that office were me, Jo and her dad. I hadn't told my parents. They thought I was going into town to look for new clothes. The only way the Greenhills could know was if they were having me followed 24/7.

I swung around, scanning the pavements behind me as I walked. There was nobody there. I was just being paranoid. If they thought I was *that* much of a threat, and they were as determined to maintain a cover-up as I suspected, they could simply have had me snatched off the street, couldn't they? The fact that I was still here, free to investigate, must surely indicate that I didn't bother them all that much!

No matter which way I looked at it, I kept coming back to the idea that one of the Greenhills was insane and that the others were hiding it. It obviously wasn't Emma, she wouldn't have had the strength to overpower someone like the man in the park. Everything pointed to Byron, who had perhaps inherited something from his grandfather Gottfried. A faulty gene? A hormone deficiency? I didn't know enough about the subject to form a realistic opinion.

Perhaps drugs kept Byron normal most of the time. Perhaps they kept having to change his medication, as the effects of one drug wore off when his system got used to it.

Perhaps this might explain their doping in Priory Mews. Perhaps they used their immediate neighbours as guinea pigs, as if they were lab rats, testing new control drugs so that when Byron – or whoever – needed new medication, it was ready.

That made a nasty kind of sense, didn't it?

When I got home, I found Mum and Dad in a positively bubbly mood. Mum was hoovering, and Dad was lifting his feet up to let Mum hoover under them.

"Did you buy anything?" said Mum.

"No," I said.

"You can go in the expensive shops now, you know."

"I know."

Mum switched off the Hoover. "How are you getting on with Emma over the road?"

"Didn't you ask me that already?" I grumbled.

"I'm asking you again."

"Fine. We get on fine."

"I'm so pleased," said Mum, squeezing up her shoulders and face in an 'ahhh' gesture. Then she nodded towards the mantelpiece above the gas fire.

There was a large white rectangle of card propped up against one of Dad's ornaments. I picked the card up and read it twice. It was an invitation, for the following Saturday, November 2nd, to attend the Annual Greenhill Family Halloween Ball at Bierce Priory, Priory Mews, Maybrick Road, Hadlington at 8pm.

RSVP.

Chapter Seven

I don't know what it was that drew me to keep watch at the back of the house on the night after we got the invitation. It was possibly nothing more than the nagging doubts that were haunting me. More likely, Martin's advice about gathering evidence was still foremost in my mind, but without any firm idea of how to go about it, simply watching and waiting seemed as useful a strategy as any.

I set up a webcam to watch the front of the Priory from my bedroom. I watched the back, from what was still a spare and as-yet-unused bedroom, on the rear corner of our house opposite my own room. I could see across our back garden, and all the way down the hill to the river. Beyond that was the park and, slightly tucked away to the right, the edge of the Elton Gardens estate.

I kept the lights off, and had a pair of binoculars and a camera with me. The image from the webcam glowed on the laptop at my feet. It was gone eleven o'clock. Mum and Dad had gone to bed, and I sat on an old fold-out chair with my elbows propped up on the window sill.

There were a few lights visible in the park. Lamps lit the cycle lanes that skirted the main lawns, and in the distance was the illuminated sign outside the leisure centre. A sickly glow came from the direction of the estate, the street lights and house lights mingling into a dull, orange-yellow shine. Now and again, you could see a glitter of light reflecting off the black surface of the river. These occasional glitters were all there was to remind you that it wasn't some gaping, bottomless trench down there. The waters sloughed along, cold and heavy, like a fat and hungry snake sliding through the landscape.

The path leading down to the river, the one that led from Maybrick Road to the green metal footbridge, was almost unlit. It was only when my eyes adjusted to the gloom that I could see it at all. An icy night mist was beginning to form in the dip where the river lay. Very gradually, it started to thicken, to creep up the hill and across the park.

I'd been sitting there watching the darkness for

about an hour before I thought of packing it in and going to bed. I hadn't seen a single living soul, or heard a sound. The sombre tranquillity of it all was somehow reassuring, though. My thoughts drifted off, until they came full circle and froze around the subject of school, and the people in it, and the endless bloody homework on my schedule.

Give it half an hour, I thought. Maybe this wasn't a good idea after all. I was getting tired and yawning.

I didn't realize it was them, at first. I caught sight of two people walking slowly down the hill, along the path. It was about a quarter past midnight now.

I picked up my binoculars to take a closer look. It was only when I'd scanned around for a few seconds, twisting the focus dial first one way and then the other, that I could see clearly. One was taller than the other, the taller one in a dark overcoat, and the other with a hood pulled tight.

It was Emma and her grandfather, Ken Greenhill. I was sure of it. Over the weeks, Emma's body language had imprinted itself on me, the same way you can identify a close friend or a member of your family at a distance, by the way they walk or the way they move their head. I was all but certain that

I could see Emma's rolling, almost gliding motion. And that semi-march of the person beside her was definitely her grandfather. Wasn't it? I could make out the walking stick swinging at his heels.

If either of them had been on their own, I'd have been less sure. As I couldn't see their faces, one of them alone wouldn't have grabbed my attention so firmly. But the two of them together made me scramble for the camera.

I put the camera on full zoom, but I couldn't get a decent image of them that way, not at such a distance and in low light. I held the camera lens against the binoculars and tried to home in on them that way, as if I had one of those large telephoto attachments. I clicked a dozen or more pictures, but flicking through them afterwards showed little more than motion blur and two vague figures in mid-stride.

As I watched them through the binoculars, I could see that Emma was carrying something. It looked like a large box with a handle, and it took me a minute or two to realize that it was a cat box. It wasn't a particularly large one but it had something in it – the way Emma was carrying it, it looked like it weighed at least a couple of kilos.

I was fully awake now, the binoculars pressed tightly to my eyes. Emma and her grandfather walked down the path, along the flat area close to the river, over the footbridge, and away to the right, into Elton Gardens. I caught a slightly sharper glimpse of them just before they moved out of sight, because they walked under one of the park's lamps and for a second they were lit up much more.

When they'd gone, I checked the time. 12:22 a.m.

What were they doing over there? When were they coming back?

I kept the binoculars trained on that patch of light beneath the lamp. They would have to pass it again, if they were going to return home the same way.

I waited, hardly daring to breathe. I kept glancing at the clock screensaver on my phone. 12:29... 12:36... 12:41...

Several times I almost gave up. I thought they must have been on their way to somewhere up in town, and I wouldn't see them again. But then I wondered where they could possibly have been going, the two of them, at that hour of the night.

It was nearly ten minutes past one when they

came back. By then, I was so used to staring at an empty patch in the distance that I didn't consciously register them until they were almost past the glow of the park lamp. I started with surprise, losing sight of them completely until I could refocus the binoculars.

They were heading home. Emma was still carrying the cat box, and it appeared to contain the same weighty object it had when they first set out. Both of them had more of a spring in their step this time, like a couple of kids hurrying as innocently as possible from the scene of a prank. I still couldn't see their faces – Emma's was shielded by her hood and the broad collar of her grandfather's overcoat was turned up against the cold. Within a couple of minutes, they had vanished into the darkness close to the top of the hill.

I watched again at the same time the following night, but saw nothing. The night after, I swapped places with the webcam.

I didn't see anything else for the rest of the week. Emma was her usual self at school, chatty and friendly. On the Thursday, she asked if my parents and I were coming to the Halloween Ball on Saturday, and I said yes, we were, and that I was really looking forward to it. She beamed at me and said she was glad. I was indeed looking forward to it, because it would give me a chance to finally see inside the Priory, and take a closer look at the Greenhills in their own home.

On the Friday, that week's *Hadlington Courier* reported that a middle-aged man had been found dead in his flat in Elton Gardens, where he lived alone. His body had been discovered on the previous day after council pest-control officers had been called to the building, when neighbours saw rats on the communal stairs and detected an odd smell coming from behind the man's front door.

He'd been dead for several days. Jo, her face wrinkled up in theatrical disgust, told me that her dad had missed out a number of details from his *Courier* report, which to save its readers' delicate sensibilities had said that the corpse was simply in a 'state of decomposition'. It had been feasted on by the rats. Most of its organs had gone, and the flesh on its head and neck had been largely stripped away.

The police did not suspect foul play. The pest-control officers dealt with the rats. An editorial in the *Courier* tut-tutted at the lack of community spirit in the area, that this poor man could lie dead, unnoticed by those who lived around him.

Chapter Eight

On Saturday night, an hour before the start of the Greenhill's Halloween Ball, my mum and dad seemed almost as cheerful and chirpy as they did on the day we moved in. Mum was wearing a black dress she'd bought specially for the occasion. Dad had dug out his old grey suit to wear, but Mum had made him give it to a charity shop and buy a new one. He came home with a suit that was almost identical to the old one.

Mum had responded to the line on the invitation that said 'Fancy Dress Optional, But Encouraged' by adding a feathered black eye mask to her dress and leaving it at that. Dad spiked his hair, painted his face black and white and said he was a rock star I'd never heard of.

I wore the zombie outfit I'd used at a school party the previous year. I had a pair of trousers with ragged edges, a shirt covered in fake gore, and a jacket with bullet holes and streams of painted blood down the back. I darkened round my eyes and put a scar across my cheek. I looked pretty good.

Cars began to fill up Priory Mews, as well as the driveway to Bierce Priory itself, about five minutes before eight o'clock. Most of them were huge and freshly cleaned. They were parked in any and every space large enough to accommodate them, and disgorged a steady stream of werewolves, mummies, pirates, monsters, witches and ghosts, as well as a scattering of dinner suits and ball gowns.

We came out of the house to find a Range Rover blocking our drive, and a pair of Hyundai iX35s pulled up on to the grass in front of our garden fence.

"Polite," I sneered.

"Oh, it doesn't matter," said Mum, to whom it would normally have mattered enormously.

It was a bitterly cold evening, the chilliest of the year so far. There was very little cloud, and the stars surrounded a bright and almost full moon.

Over at No. 1, the Daltons called goodnight to their babysitter and followed us across the road. I felt an odd shudder of cold as I stepped on to the gravel driveway of Bierce Priory. I realized it was the first time I'd actually been down their drive towards the house. Parked at the far end were a couple of large vans that had arrived earlier in the day filled with catering equipment and supplies. Mum had watched it all from our front window, keeping up a running commentary on whatever was coming and going.

The ball was being held in the long, ground-floor art-deco annexe that jutted out from the left-hand side of the main house. A shifting pattern of coloured light swirled from inside, throwing the curved and intricate shapes of the tall windows into silhouette. The rest of the house was in darkness. It towered above us, angular and brooding. Any sensation I felt of being watched was purely my own nerves and paranoia.

Three wide, semicircular stone steps led up to a pair of patio doors in the side of the annexe. They were ajar, and opened wide as we approached.

"Richard, Ellen, welcome," said Caroline Greenhill. "Hello, Sam, I know Emma's been looking forward to having you over." Caroline was dressed as a sorceress, in a scarlet dress with trails of glitter. A pair of amber contact lenses made her eyes piercing and serpentine.

"Didn't know whether we should bring a bottle," said Mum.

Caroline laughed. "Oh, no no no, that's fine." She spotted the Daltons behind us. "Oh, hello! Lovely to see you, do come in."

We went inside, into the warm fog of chatter, music and the aromas of food and wine. The annexe was one enormous room, with a polished wood floor and big lights suspended from the ceiling, designed to match the art-deco style of their surroundings. To one end was a low stage, on which a six-piece band in dinner jackets and bow ties plucked swing and jazz classics. Half a dozen couples were already dancing, one or two doing proper jive steps.

I had to admit, this was the most impressive social event I'd ever been to in my life.

"Ooh, buffet," said Dad, pointing to the tables at the other end of the room.

Mum made a grab for the Daltons, obviously self-conscious that she knew almost nobody here. "This is lovely, isn't it?" she said to Susan Dalton.

"Yes," smiled Susan.

"Susan and I met at one of these balls," said Michael Dalton.

148

"Did you leave the babysitter your mobile number?" Susan asked him. He paused, then headed back to the driveway.

I brushed nervously at the sleeves of my zombie outfit. I was acutely aware of knowing almost nobody, too. Where was—?

"Boo!"

I almost let out a yell. Emma was suddenly beside me, nearly doubled up with mirth.

"Oh, I'm sorry!" she giggled. "Did I scare you?"

"Nooo," I said, my heart racing. "Well, yes."

She cackled. "It's the Halloween Ball, I guess you deserve a good scare!"

She was in a vampire costume. A long black wig reached halfway down her back, and her eyes were heavily made up in a sharp batwing shape. Between blood-red lips, she'd painted her teeth to make them look like fangs.

"You look fabulous," I blurted.

"Thank you," she beamed. "You look utterly gross, too."

We laughed. "Do you want a drink?" she said. "There's supposed to be a couple of waiters, but I think they're all busy with the food at the moment."

She sidled up to me. My heart raced again. "Mum says I can have wine. She thinks I wait for her permission. Want some?"

"I'm OK at the moment," I said.

"Okey dokey," she said. She twirled on the spot and skipped away, heading for the lines of wine and spirits bottles near the buffet table.

There must have been close to a hundred people in the room. I caught a glimpse of Chief Constable Leonard Greenhill, whom I recognized from that TV news report. He'd come as a convict, in baggy shirt and trousers covered in arrows and a prisoner number stitched to his chest. He was chatting with three men who each mirrored his humourless expression, and who I assumed were fellow cops. Around me was a whirl of talk, laughter and high-society networking, all of which left me to my own devices.

"Sam!" said Emma. She returned holding a large glass of red wine in one hand, and Byron Greenhill's sleeve in the other. "This is my dad!"

His costume consisted of a bloodstained white lab coat, and a pair of comedy goggle-eyed glasses. He took them off and popped them into the pocket of his lab coat. His real eyes were perfectly round, the pupils large and dark. He had a slightly bulbous face, with a pink, fleshy jaw that was smooth and buttery, and a raised, skin-coloured mole beside his mouth that seemed to give his face a permanent smirk. I understood what Jo's dad had meant when he'd said that Byron Greenhill gave some people the creeps.

He spoke with the same swagger as his father Ken, the same tone of assumed superiority. "I've been hearing a lot about you, Sam," he said.

I tried to think of something witty to say, but failed completely.

"He's only just got back from... Where was it?" said Emma.

"Prague." He gazed at me levelly. "Conference. Well, nice to meet you, young man."

I felt as if I'd been dismissed, like a fly being swatted to one side. Byron Greenhill's attention was already elsewhere, zoning in on a small group of women dressed as witches.

"Those are all governors of our school," whispered Emma. Her breath was scented with the red wine. "Are you sure you wouldn't like a glass of virgin's blood?"

"Could I, umm, use your loo?" I said.

"Yeah," she said, nodding to a small door beside the buffet table. "Through there."

"Thanks."

As I drew level with the buffet table, I glanced back around the room. I spotted Ken Greenhill for the first time, bobbing gently in time to the music, in the company of the Giffords from No. 2. Mum had attached herself to a circle of business types and was laughing too loudly. Dad was standing beside the band, two young women hanging off his every word. He was tapping his foot and nodding his head, and very clearly telling them about his glittering career in showbiz. The two young women kept looking at each other.

Nobody was looking my way. Smoothly, I took a tall wine glass from the table and went through the door Emma had indicated.

Beyond was a short corridor. On the left were two further doors, each with a sign written in black marker pen on an A4 sheet: 'Gents' and 'Ladies'. At the end of the corridor was another door, which must have led into the main part of the house. I quickly went over to it.

I was hunting for evidence, of course, but exactly what that evidence might amount to, or where it might be, I didn't know. I was planning on playing it by ear.

There was a keypad built into the jamb, level with the handle. On the inner parts of the entire frame, I could see the edges of metal reinforcements. A cold feeling began to creep down my spine. This was more than ordinary security. This was hardly the sort of thing you expected to find inside someone's *home*. Unless that someone had plenty to hide.

There was a scuffling sound behind me, and I quickly ducked into the Gents. I heard the laughing chatter of two female voices, and the bumping of the Ladies door.

The temporary Gents was a large domestic shower room, with a separate toilet cubicle built into the corner. In here, the noise of the band and the people sounded hollow and distant, and the glare of the overhead light threw hard shadows across the tiled floor.

I placed the wine glass beside the hand basin. Out of the pocket of my jacket I took two lunchbox cartons of orange juice I'd brought from home. I tore the plastic straw from one of them, pierced both cartons and emptied the contents into the wine glass. The orange juice reached the rim of the glass, and I bent down to slurp it back a little. I dumped the cartons in the little pedal bin under the basin.

It would have looked odd if I hadn't eaten or drunk anything. I had planned, before leaving home, that this glass was going to stay in my hand for the duration of the party. I wouldn't put it down, not for a second. I would sip it occasionally, and claim it was one of those things that's made with orange juice – what was it called? A spritzer? No, a Buck's Fizz.

If Dr Caroline Greenhill had wanted me to attend her surgery, then she'd been planning to drug me just like the rest of Priory Mews. There was no way I was going to let anyone slip me dope in a crustless sandwich or a tumbler of lemonade. I wasn't going to fall for that.

I wasn't going to get into the main part of the house either. Not with that code-locked door there.

I took a deep breath, had a sip of orange juice, and strode back out into the main room with my glass firmly in my hand. The band was kicking up the tempo. Most of the guests were dancing, the others watching them. Werewolves and vampires, monsters and ghouls, spectres and aliens, swaying and waltzing and dad-dancing. The early atmosphere of stylish formality had loosened a little.

Emma found me and we danced, too, awkwardly. My glass stayed in my hand. Emma's glass stayed in hers. She'd pause here and there to slug some red wine back. There was raucous applause when the band finished a song and announced they'd be taking a short break. Emma and I found a couple of seats, on their own beside one of the annexe's immensely tall windows.

"This is a beautiful room," I said, looking up at the ornate details of the high ceiling.

"It's been in the family for about seventy years," said Emma. "Just like my grandpop's jokes."

I fought back the urge to ask her where she'd been going the previous Sunday night. "Are we the youngest ones here?" I said.

Emma nodded. "By at least a decade."

"Don't you get to invite some of your friends?"

She wrinkled her nose. "No, it's Mum and Dad's thing, really. Anyway, you're here, you're my friend. It's not so much a party, it's more a sort of mixture of a thank you and a … what's the word I want? I was going to say bribe, but that's not right."

"Bribe?" I said, eyebrows raised.

"No, not bribe. These people are all council leaders, school governors, police officers, Dad's science guys, Mum's medical guys, well, both of their medical guys."

She sort of giggled to herself. I thought the wine was starting to go to her head.

"The best and brightest of Hadlington, and beyond," she continued. "And Mum and Dad like to stay best friends with all of them. Well, why not? If you're going to have friends, have the best. Anyway, it's a thank you and a … whatever. For being best friends, and for … carrying on being best friends. You wait until you see the goodie bags everyone gets at the end."

"There are goodie bags?"

"Ah!" said Emma. "The good news is, yes, there are goodie bags. The bad news is, Mum does them, they're all named, and the people they want to be bestest, bestest ever BFF buddies get the biggest pressies. I'm afraid the neighbours have to make do with chocolates and the odd bottle or two."

"Chocolates are nice," I shrugged.

Many of the guests were standing around with

plates, filling their faces and burying themselves in conversations. Byron and Caroline were working the room, shaking hands and kissing cheeks and sharing light banter – 'pressing the flesh' as the politicians put it. A photographer had turned up, presumably from the *Courier*. White flashes popped in the far corner of the room. There'd be a couple of pics in next week's issue, showing the Greenhills and assorted dignitaries smiling and having fun.

"I'm glad the Daltons didn't bring their horrible squealing brat," said Emma.

"I think they got a babysitter."

"Yeah?" said Emma. "I hope she strangles the little shit."

I flinched. I assumed that was the wine talking.

Mum and Dad were together, Mum hanging around near the photographer and not being invited to appear in a group shot, Dad standing behind her happily tucking into a plate that was piled high. I was sure that was his third. I caught a trio of nearby vampires eyeing the pair of them, exchanging hushed remarks and sniggering to themselves. A flush of anger welled up inside me.

The band finished pints of beer and hopped back

up on to the stage. The music resumed with a rapid beat from the drummer and a catchy melody from the guy on the electric piano. Dad put down his plate and yanked Mum into a twirling dance that mimicked a waltz so badly that the business types Mum had been talking to earlier all clapped and laughed.

Whatever embarrassment I felt suddenly melted as Emma slid across and nestled up to me. She rested her cheek on my shoulder, and her leg was pressed against mine. My head turned, and I was looking directly into her large, everlasting eyes.

"Shall we have another dance in a minute?" she whispered.

"OK," I said.

Her blood-red lips parted slowly. I felt an unbidden urge to kiss her. Even then, when I already had suspicions, her pull was almost irresistible.

"Do you think vampires and zombies get on well?" she whispered. "Do you think they ever have an undead romance?"

I smiled. "I expect your average zombie would just try to eat a vampire. And I shouldn't think zombie blood tastes very nice."

Her fake fangs glittered as the music swayed. "I'll take the risk," she muttered.

A loud group belly laugh burst out close by. I snapped my gaze aside to see Chief Inspector Leonard Greenhill's group of cops guffawing amongst themselves.

I saw one of them pull a handkerchief from his pocket. He snatched at his nose, wiping away the thin, yellowish trail that had been there.

My heart froze. So it wasn't only the people in Priory Mews. There were others. Was this man a patient of Caroline Greenhill, too? Of course he was, he had to be.

The next thing I knew, I could see Emma walking away, my sight of her quickly blocked by dancers. I dumbly glanced at the empty space beside me, as if I expected to see her in two places at once.

I squeezed my eyes shut for a moment. I hoped she hadn't thought my switch of attention was deliberate; that I was snubbing her. With a sigh, I finished my orange juice. There was almost half of it left. My hand had warmed it up in the glass and it tasted peculiar.

I was getting weary of the crowd, and the tempo of the music. I watched the forest of bodies shifting around the floor. I wondered how much accumulated wealth this gathering represented.

I saw Mum and Dad jigging about and the anger I'd felt earlier flooded back. It was as if these people could smell poverty on us. I felt like a trained monkey, being exhibited for their amusement.

I don't know how much time passed but finally Byron and Caroline Greenhill were beside the doors, next to a large table that had been set up, filled with sparkly gold gift bags. Gradually the guests decided it was time to make a move, told casual acquaintances how lovely it'd been to catch up, said we mustn't leave it so long next time.

Byron and Caroline handed out gift bags. Pecks on the cheek, firm shakes of the hand. Nobody had the vulgarity to look inside the bags. See you next week, see you at work, see you at the club, see you when I get back.

The cold seemed to seep into the room like a grey, creeping mist. Tendrils slithered across the floor. I could almost hear it.

I *could* hear it. A slow, rasping wheeze, like the dying exhalation of a gigantic reptile. I looked around, but it seemed to be coming from everywhere at once. I stood up, and walked over to where Mum and Dad were talking with the Giffords.

"Are you ready to go, Sam?" chirped Mum. Her voice was slightly louder than all those around her. "Hasn't it been a lovely party?"

"Lovely," smiled Mrs Gifford. She tapped at the top button of her dress.

"Aren't you going to say goodbye to Emma?" said Mum.

"Umm…"

I couldn't see her anywhere.

Dad slapped me on the back. "Time to hit the road, sonny jim."

Then we were at the doors. "Great party, man," Dad said to Byron.

Byron grinned at him indulgently. Mum hovered, glancing towards the table of goodie bags. Caroline picked through the ones that remained.

"Ah, Mr and Mrs Gifford," she said, lifting a couple of them clear, "do please accept these, just a small token of friendship for our neighbours… Not at all… Now, then … Ellen and Richard and Sam… Here we are. Happy Halloween, all."

"Thank you so much," said Mum, peeking into

her bag. "It's been a wonderful evening."

Caroline beamed warmly at her. "Yes. Yes, it has."

"Goodnight," said Byron, with a nod.

"Nighty night," said Mum.

Then we were crunching along the driveway of Bierce Priory. The light from the annexe spilled out into the night, casting our shadows into grotesque shapes in front of us.

I could hear it again!

Slithering. Movement in the bushes. A regular, pulsing hiss of weight against fallen leaves.

"What's that?"

"What's what, Sam?" said Dad.

"Aren't the Greenhills lovely people?" said Mum.

"Salt of the earth," said Mr Gifford, arm in arm with his wife.

"It's nice to see people in, y'know, a privileged position giving something back," said Dad. "To the community."

"They've been very generous to our church's restoration fund," said Mrs Gifford.

"Shh!" I hissed. "Can't you hear it?"

Dad made an exaggerated hand-to-ear listening pose. "Nope."

I kept looking over my shoulder. There was nobody there. Nobody, nothing, just the Priory.

Yet, it was creeping up on us. It was hidden away, it was sneaking through the undergrowth, crawling under the gravel. Watching us, stalking us, licking its fangs!

I could hear it. Closer, closer. Its thin lips dripping.

"What *is* that? Listen! Listen!"

"That Caroline is a terrific woman," mumbled Dad.

We walked out into the road. Most of the cars were gone. One of the Hyundais was still parked on our grass.

The grass. Safe. It wouldn't come out on to the grass, not where we could see it. It had to stay back, in the shadows.

I would stay on the grass. The grass that was growing. Up, around, over, always growing, growing, growing. Through cracks in the pavement. All over. Growing into the air, the ground, the buildings, out of the mouths of the people.

I shook my head. Thoughts seemed to cram and jumble around my mind, a senseless mess. I felt strange, disconnected.

"Are you all right, Sam?"

"Yes, I'm fine."

Inside the house. Home. Mum and Dad went to put the kettle on.

I felt shaky and vacant, as if bits and pieces of me were falling away. Nothing quite seemed to fit. I tried to hold things in my head, one after the other, but they dissolved, like sand running through my fingers.

Suddenly, without any kind of warning, I was furious.

This wasn't right. Something was happening to me. No, something had been done to me. It was them.

I marched into the kitchen. I heard words come out of me, but couldn't connect them with anything in my brain. "How can you not see what's going on? The Greenhills, they're *evil*!"

Dad narrowed his eyes at me. "Have you been at the wine gums?"

"Sam?" said Mum.

"I thought Emma looked a little worse for wear," chuckled Dad. "Were you both on the vino?"

"*No!*" I shouted. The sound bounced off the walls. They both flinched.

"I think you'd better get to bed," said Mum quietly.

"I'm sorry," I said. "But can't you see? They've … to me…" What? Done what?

Nothing made… What?

I was at the foot of the stairs. I was halfway up the stairs. I was in my room.

It seemed peaceful. Warm and quiet. The only light was the faint glow of the moon. I went into my bathroom, then got undressed and got into bed.

I was safe here, in my bed, under the covers. They wouldn't get me here, nothing could get me tucked up in my own little bed. No, not here, not here, not here.

Then suddenly something snapped at me! Out of the darkness! Up from under the covers. The thing from outside. Red eyes, and sharp teeth, clambering up me, clacking its jaws, dribbling. Its claws dug into me, sharp, climbing up towards my head.

I screamed, and it was gone.

But my scream woke the bugs. Millions, billions, legs and antennae. Scuttering and scuttling. Squeezing up through the floorboards, millions, billions, trillions. Buzzing and chittering, spreading out like a crawling carpet, gushing, flooding, bursting, filling the house, filling the bath, filling my room. Deeper and deeper, a sea of oozing thoraxes and abdomens.

I couldn't move. The insects scrambled over my bed, between the sheets, through my pillow. They bit me, smothering me from hair to toenails. They burrowed and dug, eating, eating, eating, sliding beneath my skin.

I was eaten away. And the bugs ate themselves. And there was nothing.

I stared up at the ceiling, wild-eyed. Silent. Still.

Many, many minutes. Still. Silent.

The white ceiling was a dark grey, with a lighter set of rectangles to one side where the moon shone through the window. For a while, there was peace again.

Gradually, the lighter rectangles of light moved. They distorted. They stretched. And then they retreated, returning to their original shape.

But it wasn't the light that was moving. It was the ceiling. The ceiling was breathing. Slowly, in and out, gently up and down, regular and steady, right above my head.

A dark spot appeared, directly in my line of sight. A flake of plaster spiralled down and landed on the bedclothes, beside my face. The spot grew, wider and longer. There was a slight tearing sound, like someone slowly ripping a sheet of paper in two.

The plaster of the ceiling peeled back. It blossomed and curled, like a speeded-up film of a flower opening. The spot became a hole, the hole widened into a gap. Behind it, nothing but an inky, light-swallowing blackness.

Out of the blackness flowered a mass, a seething, spotted growth of animal tissue, diseased and eaten, rotting away, spreading out across the ceiling. The remnants of me, of the insects.

Down through the mass heaved a lump. A shape, pushing through the twisting, peeling skin of it. The mass suddenly split. Blood and pus leaked sideways along the rip.

Then a face emerged, streaked with blood. Emma's. Her eyes red, her lips smiling.

The face grew, bloated, expanded. She opened her mouth. It became a chasm, stretching out and back, folding her head away, revealing a huge, glistening hand beneath.

The hand folded, in order to fit its stick-like fingers through the encrusted, peeled opening in the ceiling. Each finger ended in a jagged, pointed claw. The fingers spread as the hand descended. Between the bony fingers, in the palm of the hand, grew something dark and wriggling. Slimy, beating cilia fluttering from the growth's wrinkled, collapsed surface.

The hand reached closer, down, down. Around it floated a yellowing mist. It groped for my face, its fingers stretching, claws slicing the air. Like a giant spider, legs folding and flexing. Reaching for my face, to dig into it, to cut it, to tear it off, to pop out my eyeballs, to pull away my skin and muscles and sinews, to leave my skull howling in the night.

A scream dried raw in my throat.

Not real, not real, not real, I said to myself over, and over, and over, and over.

My reeling mind struggled to steady itself.

They'd drugged me. I couldn't even form the concept in my head at that moment, but some tiny part of myself said that they had drugged me.

Emma had drugged me, when she got close. It had all been an act. The words, the lips. She'd put something in my glass. *Emma* had drugged me.

168

Chapter Nine

For hours, the horrible visions persisted. One folded into another, sending horrible creatures running for me, leaping at me. I kept shutting my eyes, but the things would crawl beneath my eyelids. I could feel sticky breath against my neck, forked tongues licking at my chin.

I lay as still as I could. I tried to concentrate on what I could see through my window, or across my room, until they too warped into hideous pulsing blossoms. Filth! Infection!

Terrified to cry out, or get up, I waited for the nightmare to end. Just a nightmare, I chanted to myself. They caused it. Emma caused it. It's just a nightmare, with a cause, and an effect, and it will end. It will end.

I had no sense of time. When the first glints of daylight showed at my window, I was as surprised as if they'd been there when I got home.

It was close to half past ten that morning, Sunday, before I sat up in bed, trembling and weak. My head ached. Shadows still scuttled through my mind, but somehow I could get a better grip of it now. I believed myself, when I said it wasn't real.

After another hour or so, I was sure that the worst had passed. Whatever they'd dosed me with, its effects were subsiding. I swung my legs out and sat on the edge of the bed, cradling my splitting head in my hands. I fought back a wave of tears.

I'd wanted to give Emma the benefit of the doubt. Until I was sitting there, on the side of the bed, I'd wanted to believe that, somehow, Emma was on the periphery of whatever the Greenhills were doing.

No more. She wasn't reluctantly hiding a family evil, or acting under duress, or the one innocent person caught up in a terrible secret. The tipsiness was all a fake, presumably. She'd drugged me like an expert, efficiently and with a smile, distracting me with her eyes and her touch.

Whatever uncertain feelings I'd had for her were gone now. They were turned to stone.

But why had she done it?

The answer was as blindingly obvious as my

headache. The Greenhills wanted to warn me off. They wanted to deliver a clear message to me: keep out of our business. We can deal with you at any time we like. You are marked. Keep quiet, shut up, or suffer the consequences.

I felt a nauseating mixture of terror and thrill. Terror at their threat, and at knowing they were on to me. Oddly thrilled at the prospect that I'd been right. There was something evil about them. There was no question about it now.

If they'd planned to drug me, why not give me whatever they gave to Mum and Dad, and the others – something pacifying? I reasoned that their 'medication' for the others must be something that you had to keep taking, that had to build up and be maintained over time, hence those regular so-called check-ups. One shot of it wouldn't have had enough effect on my system. They needed to frighten me, badly enough to stop me in my tracks.

They must have been on the alert ever since that night when I saw the dog and the face at the window. They had brand-new neighbours that night, undrugged neighbours, and when that scream rang out they must have known there was a chance we'd heard it. That was why Caroline had turned up on our doorstep next morning. To check. And I had told them, *myself*, that I'd heard something!

It slowly dawned on me that I'd been wrong about one thing: somehow, they must have known about my visit to Jo's dad at the *Courier*. They wouldn't have drugged me like that if they'd only suspected I *might* cause a problem, if they were only keeping tabs on me. They knew I'd been investigating them: they really did see me as a threat, and not merely a *potential* troublemaker. The only thing that could have led them to believe that was my meeting in town.

Summoning up what was left of my strength, I showered, dressed and called Jo.

The minute she came to the phone, I could tell from her voice that something was up. "Are you OK?" I said.

"We've just got back from the hospital."

"What? Why?"

"My dad had a heart attack yesterday. He's OK, he's out of danger and everything, but my mum and me are still a bit … shaky, y'know?"

"I'm so sorry," I said. "He's going to be all right, though?"

"Yes, they said it could have been a lot worse, but he's got wires all over him and they're going to keep him in for a few days."

"How are you?"

"Well, a bundle of nerves, but better than yesterday."

"That's awful. He seemed fine last week."

"Oh, Mum's been telling him to lose weight for years. She's been nagging him that he's one pork pie away from a stroke, and she was right. Stupid sod. He's going to be on nothing but salad when he gets home. Before I forget, he had a message for you."

"What? For me?"

"Yes," said Jo. "I was going to tell you at school tomorrow, but... Anyway, he said to tell you that from your conversation with him last week, scenario one now looks the most reasonable. I don't know what he's on about."

I frowned. "Er, yes, I know what he means."

"You sound a bit shaky yourself?"

I paused. "No, no, I'm fine. Just shocking news, you know."

"I'll see you tomorrow."

"See you."

I sat in silence for a minute or two. Conflicting emotions went to war inside me.

I had been drugged, Jo's dad was in the hospital. His message indicated that he now believed my suspicions about the Greenhills were correct. Which implied that his heart attack was as much their fault as my doping. How, I couldn't begin to guess.

I felt cold and frightened. Just how far did their network extend? Just how powerful were they?

Once again, I was plagued with thoughts of giving up. It would have been so much easier to toe the line.

But I've never responded to threats. Or to bullies. That chip on my shoulder kept me defiant.

I went downstairs, leaning against the bannisters. I was still slightly unsteady on my feet.

"Look what the cat dragged in," said Dad. He was stretched out on the sofa, sections of the Sunday newspaper spread out around him on the floor.

"You look white as a sheet," tutted Mum. "Were you drinking last night?"

"No."

"It's OK, you can tell us, we won't be cross. It's covering it up that'd make me cross."

"Mum, I had one glass of orange juice. I swear."

"Then why are you so pale?" she said softly, holding the sides of my face in her hands.

I nearly blubbed again. "I didn't sleep much. I've got a headache, that's all."

She smoothed a hand across my hair, the way she used to when I was little, and off school with a bug. She smiled at me and kissed my forehead. I couldn't remember the last time she'd been that way with me. But there it was again, now that she was doped up to the eyeballs.

I felt lousy for most of the rest of the day. All I did was slump in front of the telly, stewing in my own worries and ignoring the homework I needed to finish. I went to bed early, more tired than I could ever remember being, and slept like a log. Like the dead.

The following morning, Monday, I overslept and was almost late again. At least school was only a few hundred metres from my front door. I'd perfected the art of going from bed to classroom in fourteen minutes flat.

I saw Jo in the corridors and gave her a hug. Liam hadn't heard about the heart attack, so he gave her an even bigger hug. She told us she was fine. She'd popped in to see her dad on the way to school, and he'd seemed a lot brighter.

In the pre-bell rush, there wasn't time to tell them about Saturday. When they asked what the Greenhills' Halloween Ball was like, all I said was, "OK. Long story."

I saw Emma, too, from a distance. Here she was, carrying on as normal – totally as normal. As if nothing had happened. She was so much her usual self that I started to doubt my own sanity, asking myself for a split second if I'd got it wrong. *But then,* I thought, *she's probably expecting me to be cowering and silent now, to be wary of her, and afraid.*

Purely by chance, our paths crossed at lunchtime. Emma was heading for a table, just as I was leaving. When she caught sight of me, she smiled, then blushed and glanced down.

"Hi, Sam,"

"Hello," I said politely.

"I really have to apologize," she said, biting the side of her bottom lip. "I, er, had a bit too much of that red wine on Saturday night. I, er, might have given you the wrong impression. I'm really sorry."

She glowed with sincerity and warmth. She expected her radiance and good looks to enslave me, even today, even after what she'd done!

Fury clouded my judgement. That chip on my shoulder.

Say it! Say it!

"I know what you did," I said, my voice trembling only slightly.

She smiled her perfect, beautiful smile. She placed a hand on my shoulder and leaned against me on tiptoe, her lips a millimetre from my ear. She spoke in a delicate whisper. "So be a good boy, and do as you're told."

Her words chilled my blood. She stood back, her smile still in place. In her eyes – those eyes – was a glint of sharpened steel.

I'm sure my face betrayed my horror. I hoped she'd interpret it as compliance.

"I-I will," I lied.

She winked at me, and went on her way.

As we left school at the end of the day, I finally brought Liam and Jo up to date on everything that had been happening. All I left out was the meaning of Jo's dad's message to me. I didn't want her to be even more upset about his condition.

Liam was still sceptical. "This is conspiracy theory stuff," he said. "Although, I have to admit, having coded locks and security doors inside *is* pretty odd. Jo's dad is right, you need proper evidence."

"Emma bloody well drugged him!" hissed Jo.

"He thinks. He didn't see it happen," said Liam.

"Oh, so, where did the hallucinations come from?"

"I'm not saying she didn't," said Liam. "I'm saying you need actual, physical, in-your-hand evidence."

"And I intend to get it," I said.

"How?" said Liam.

"As far as I can see, there's only one option left," I said. "None of the Greenhills are ever likely to let direct evidence get out into the open. Agreed? They're far too clever for that."

"Yes," said Liam.

"Which includes Emma's mum not leaving supplies of suspect drugs at her surgery, her dad not carrying anything suspicious on trips, all that sort of thing. Agreed?"

"Probably, yes," said Liam.

"And we know they keep the house locked up tight. So if there's evidence to be found, that's where it'll be. That's where we've got to look. I have to get into Bierce Priory."

They both stared at me for a moment.

"You mean break in?" said Liam.

"Well, I don't mean knock on the front door and ask to root through their wardrobes!"

"That *is* a crime," said Jo. "You *are* aware of that."

"Give me an alternative," I said, throwing my arms wide.

"Tell the cops?" said Jo.

"With Leonard Greenhill in charge of every police officer for miles?" I said.

"Tell school?" said Liam. "Ah, no, stupid idea, I can answer my own question there."

"School procedures would send the Head straight to the cops *and* Emma's parents," said Jo. "Sam would be totally sunk."

"Yeah, I realized as soon as I said it," said Liam, holding his hands up.

Terrifying thoughts about what I might find inside the Priory flashed through my mind. "I just can't see another way," I said.

I got a call at about seven that evening from Jo's dad, Martin. He'd been discharged from the hospital that afternoon, and had arrived home shortly after Jo got back from school.

"Hi! Are you OK?" I said.

"Fighting fit," he said. He lowered his voice a little. "Although I've only been home two hours and already I've had a bar of chocolate snatched out of my hand. Anyway, look, I'm calling to tell you two things. One, you were right."

"I heard."

"You know why? On Saturday, we had a visitor at work. Byron Greenhill. There were about half a dozen of us in the office. He turned up carrying cappuccinos from the coffee shop downstairs."

"What did he want?"

"To ask if we were going to send a photographer to cover the Halloween Ball that night."

I frowned. "Don't you always? Why didn't he just phone?"

"Exactly," said Jo's dad. "He was telling us a funny story about how he'd flown in from Eastern

180

Europe, somewhere, at the crack of dawn, and how some jobsworth at the airport had nearly shredded his passport. I was wondering why, after a tiring journey, he'd bothered to come into town when he could have called, but like everyone else in the office I was standing there, listening to him, chuckling along, sipping my cappuccino, like a prize idiot."

"Why like an idiot?"

"Because of what you'd shown me. If he'd turned up a couple of weeks ago, I'd have thought nothing of it. Nothing at all. Just a local bigwig popping in to make sure he gets a grip-and-grin in the next issue, for a bit of PR. But since this particular bigwig turns up on this particular day, alarm bells ring. Because of your research."

"In what way?" I said, feeling increasingly nervous.

"*Why's he standing around amusing us with stories,* I think to myself. *He's got a party to organize, he must have things to do. We're not his mates from the Chamber of Commerce or the County Council. What's with all the coffee and buddy-buddy stuff?* And then a nasty little thought hits me. He's waiting."

"For what?"

"He's waiting for us to drink the coffee. Or, perhaps, he's waiting for *me* to drink the coffee. I get a heads-up that one of the Greenhills might be a serious nutcase, and lo and behold, the chief suspect turns up bearing gifts. Do you see what I'm getting at?"

I didn't mention what had happened to me after the party. I guessed that Jo had already told him.

"You don't think he heard about our meeting from me, do you?" I said.

"No, no, no, of course not. The man's a social octopus, he'll have tentacles everywhere. Anyway, as soon as I thought that, I didn't touch another drop. I hadn't had much of it. He leaves a few minutes later, all smiles and thank yous, my colleagues say what a great bloke he is, and we all go back to work."

"What happened to the coffee? What was in it?"

"I put it down, I set it aside. I thought, first thing on Monday, I'll send it to be analyzed. Like I said, nothing of the sort would ever have occurred to me before, but after seeing your file, anything's possible. Less than two hours later, I'm in an ambulance."

"Jesus, what if you'd drunk the lot?" I cried.

"Quite," he said. "You saved my life, young man. Which leads me on to Thing To Tell You number two. When you get a chance, give Jo that file of yours, so she can pass it on to me. Don't come back into the office, yeah?"

"Yes, OK. What was in the coffee?"

"We'll never know. By the time I remembered it, after I woke up at the hospital, it was too late. I rang the office. The cleaner had been in. It was tipped away."

"That would have been evidence."

"Absolutely. And to bring it in himself like that, he's either so damned arrogant he assumes he'd never be caught, or he's desperate to stop any leaks of information. So we're still at square one on the evidence front, but once I've got your file, I'll do some digging of my own. Got to go, there's a cup of herbal tea with my name on it."

His words rattled around my head for hours. Now, more than ever, I was determined to find evidence, to prove that something was going on.

Breaking into Bierce Priory was the worst mistake of my life.

But how could I have known? How could I have foreseen what would happen?

I was blinded by my raging desire to get at the

truth. I can see that now. But I couldn't have known what the truth would cost me… Could I?

It was the next day that our fate was sealed. Although it was Thursday, it was the last day of that particular school week. The Friday was a teacher-training day, and there'd be no lessons. At break, I talked with Jo while we waited for Liam to turn up.

Then I said to both of them: "I was thinking about this half the night. I'm going to hold off handing over that file until I've got something better to include in it."

"Like what?" said Liam.

I let out a long, slow breath. "I've got to take the only option."

Liam pulled a face. "Er, hello, criminal record."

"Someone could get in there tomorrow," said Jo. "They'd have hours to look around."

"How come?" said Liam.

"I told Sam before you got here," said Jo. "Emma's going to New York in the morning. The whole family's going for a long weekend, shopping. All of them, including the grandad. They won't be back until late Sunday night. She told a couple of people in her class this morning, and now half the year's heard about it. They only decided over breakfast today. Last-minute ticket deal, apparently. This could be our perfect opportunity."

Liam's gaze darted between Jo and me. "I'm hearing 'we' and 'us' here."

"Because I'm totally with Sam on this," said Jo.

"What? Why?"

"Sam is right. The Greenhills are extremely well protected: officially, socially, legally, every way. There's no way to get to the truth from the outside; you've got to get it from the inside, or not at all."

"Whoa, whoa, whoa, and that justifies breaking the law, does it?" said Liam.

"They'll be gone all weekend," said Jo. "We get in, look around, find the evidence we need. And if there isn't any to be found, or getting to it proves impossible, then we just get out again. Nothing is left disturbed, nobody need ever know."

"I can hear that 'we' again," said Liam.

"I'm going in there with Sam," said Jo.

I was as surprised to hear this as Liam was.

Jo's lips pressed tightly together for a moment.

"Just something my dad said, OK? The Greenhills are bloody evil, trust me."

"He told you about the coffee?" I said quietly.

She nodded. "Only me. Not Mum. She'd go ape."

"What coffee?" said Liam.

We told him about the attempt on Jo's dad's life. "You see why these people have got to be brought down?" I said. "The thing is, to get into the house, I'm going… OK, *we're* going to need help. You're the technical one."

Liam saw what I was getting at immediately. "Oh, no, come on. I'll lend you some gear, but I'm not going to commit a burglary. I'm applying for university before the end of term – I'm not doing that from some young offenders' institution! And anyway, if the Greenhills are poisoning people now, what the bloody hell will they do if they catch us?"

"They'll be thousands of miles away," said Jo. "We won't get caught."

"And if we discover some real evidence, we're not going to get put in prison," I said. "We'll be heroes."

Liam held the sides of his face, in an agony of indecision. "Can't I just lend you a laptop, and wires, and a set of instructions?"

"It's not going to be that easy, is it?" I said. "Picking those electronic locks is going to need a level of technical skill that I don't have. And Jo doesn't have either."

"What if they've got cameras?" said Liam. "What if they've got motion sensors? I'm not bloody MI5! I can hack a computer system, and bypass a few security measures, but no way can I get you through something really sophisticated."

"All we've got to do is get in," I said. "We may only need a matter of minutes. If an alarm goes off, and the cops turn up, not even the Greenhills will be able to stop our evidence getting out. My guess is there's no alarm, just heavy locks."

"Based on what?" said Liam.

"They'll want that place secure, but silent. They won't have it linked up to the police, in case officers turn up who aren't part of their network. And they certainly won't have any kind of loud siren, nothing that draws attention. And if they've got a few cameras on the walls, so what? We'll have our evidence. It'll be too late for them."

Jo tugged at Liam's sleeve and flickered her eyelids

at him, putting on a jokey voice. "Help us, Obi-Liam, you're our only hope."

I could see he was burning to help her, to impress her. He looked from me to Jo and back again. "If I can't crack the first door inside two minutes, it's not happening, right?"

"Right."

"I mean it. I'm not spending half an hour writing lines of code. And if we hear barking, we leg it."

"Right, yes, understood," I said.

Sure enough, the Greenhills left the Priory at shortly after 7 a.m. the following morning. I'd set my alarm early, and watched through a narrow gap in my curtains, slowly spooning cereal from a bowl.

I watched Caroline double-lock the front door and check it. They loaded a couple of small cases into the boot of their car. Emma was almost skipping with excitement. Ken clambered into the back beside her. Byron and Caroline sat in the front, Byron driving. The growl of the car's engine was loud in the pre-dawn stillness. The headlights flicked on, throwing sharp circles of white against the windowed wall of the annexe. The Renault slowly reversed, U-turned on the road, and was away.

I phoned Liam and Jo. We arranged to meet up two hours later, once the Greenhills were safely on their way. I'd already told Mum and Dad that the three of us were working on a geography project and that we'd be out and about in the park for hours. Mum had gone to work by eight, and Dad was still gently snoring at twenty past nine. I watched for Liam and Jo from the living room, and went out to meet them as they approached.

"If we're going in through the back," said Jo, "we'll need a way to scale that fence."

"I had an idea about that last night," I said. "We can climb up on one of the bins." I turned to Liam. "Have you got everything?"

He tapped at the backpack slung over his shoulder. "I went into town after school yesterday, and got one of those home video transmitters. With a portable power pack it should scramble camera signals within a small radius. Just in case."

"Genius," I grinned.

A few minutes later, we were at the side of our

house, morning light turning the sky a washed-out semi-blue. I dragged one of our black wheelie bins out from the enclosed section behind our garden gate, where it was kept. I bumped it over the grass, to the tall metal railings that bordered the Priory's grounds. I kept shivering, although whether it was from nerves or the biting cold, I couldn't tell.

We found a spot where there was no direct line of sight to us from anywhere on the hill leading down to the river, and positioned the bin up against the fence. I almost tipped it over as I climbed up on top of it. Crouching unsteadily for a moment, I regained my balance and placed the toe of one of my chunky walking boots between two of the spikes that topped the metal railings. Then in one movement I heaved myself up on to one leg, swung forward and jumped.

I hit the grass with a painful thud. A zing of pins and needles shot through my leg. Shaking it off, I caught Liam's backpack when he threw it over. Jo was next. I caught her by the waist as she jumped, breaking her fall. We both had to break Liam's fall by grabbing his arms, as he was the tallest and heaviest of us. Liam gathered up his bag and we walked towards the Priory.

None of us said a word. The only sound was the swish of our boots on the frost-whitened grass.

I looked up at the building. As blank as an empty grave. A sense of cold loneliness surrounded the place, a strange and helpless feeling of abandonment. I quickly located the window from which that peculiar apparition had been staring at me, weeks before. The window was as dark and vacant as the rest of the house.

We approached a small, porch-like section that jutted out on to a broad, neatly kept terrace. In between two more lines of metal railings, low and narrow this time, a short set of stone steps led down to a heavy door that was set deep into the wall, half below ground level and half above.

"You'd think they'd have shutters at the windows, or something," whispered Jo.

"Too obvious, maybe," I said. "It might encourage people to think there was something in here worth nicking."

"No cameras," mumbled Liam. "I doubt they'd have hidden them, or it wouldn't be a deterrent. Typical. Now I've got the stuff to deal with them. Can you see any cameras?" We couldn't.

The stone steps were worn, most of them slightly slumped in the middle. To the right-hand side of the door was a keypad, just like the one I'd seen before. It was shielded from the elements with a curved plastic cover.

Glancing over our shoulders, we went down the steps. We huddled together in the doorway as Liam drew a laptop and an assortment of connectors from his backpack.

If someone had asked me, at that moment, what I thought we were going to find, I wouldn't have been able to say. I was trying to keep my mind and my eyes open. Maybe a cell for containing Byron – or whoever – during psychotic episodes? Or supplies of experimental drugs? Paperwork showing how the residents of Priory Mews had been doped? Clothes stained with the blood of the murder victim from the park?

There were so many possibilities. The only thing we weren't prepared for, in any way, was what we actually found.

Chapter Ten

Liam used a tiny screwdriver, the sort you find in Christmas crackers, to remove the cover from the keypad. Beneath it, the plastic number keys stood out from a small circuit board.

"That's where the power comes in," he whispered, pointing to the top left corner of the board. "And this is where the signal from the keys goes, over here." I had the feeling he was talking to himself rather than us, mostly as a way of steadying his nerves. His fingers shook slightly as he pointed.

He flipped open the laptop. Its screen showed a series of black boxes with lists of coding in green. He plugged two USB leads into the computer, and handed it to me.

"Hold this," he said quietly. "Now, these little metal rods on the other ends of these leads, what we have to do is touch the right parts of the circuit board with them, to intercept the signals going through it, and then the program on the laptop works out what the right keycode is."

He stood examining the board, ducking his head up and down, the two leads held between his fingers. The cold was biting at my face, and I shivered again. Jo had tucked her hands under her arms for warmth. I could hear Liam's breathing.

At last, Liam connected the ends of the leads to different parts of the circuit board. As soon as he did so, one of the boxes on the laptop screen began to scroll. He glanced over at it, keeping his hands as still as possible.

"OK," he muttered. "Tell me when you get an 'at' symbol followed by numbers."

A few seconds later, the flowing green codes had reduced down to: '@34516'

Liam plucked the ends of the leads away, replaced the keypad cover, and tapped 3, 4, 5, 1, 6 into it. Behind the door, there was a sudden loud click. The sound made us all jump. The laptop and leads were bundled away into Liam's bag.

"Ready?" I said. They nodded.

I took hold of the door's handle and turned it slowly. The door opened, swinging back a little on fat, squeaky hinges.

Without pausing, we moved inside. I took a look at the door's edge. There was a thin layer of metal visible from top to bottom.

"See? Security doors," I said.

"No barking," mumbled Liam.

As I closed it behind us, Jo flicked a light switch. We were in a kind of antechamber, about three metres square, with a stone floor and brick walls painted in off-white gloss. Ahead of us, a low archway led to a narrow passage. To one side was a darkened recess, holding a lawnmower and a rack of garden tools. To the other side, more stone steps went up, in a curve, until they were out of sight.

The air was absolutely still. There was a slightly musty smell, like old sacking. We didn't have to look at each other to know we were all trembling with fear.

I took a couple of paces towards the stairway. "I expect that goes up into the main part of the house," I whispered.

"What are we whispering for, there's nobody here," said Liam.

"When this place was built, down here was

probably servants' quarters," said Jo. Like Liam outside, we were talking to distract ourselves from the reality of the situation.

"What's the time?" I said.

"Nine minutes past ten," said Jo. "Their flight takes off at half past. I checked online before I left home – all flights to New York are fine, no bad weather, no strikes."

"Look again," I said.

Jo pulled her phone from her back pocket. "All fine, everything's on time. The only flights at any airport showing delays are flights to the Far East. Typhoon warning in China, it says here."

"OK, where do we begin?" said Liam.

Of course, we should have checked once more, a few minutes later, but we were too overwhelmed by our discoveries. If we'd checked again, we would have seen the word 'cancellation' come up. The Greenhills would be back in their Renault very soon, disappointed and heading for home.

We thought we had all the time in the world. We had less than an hour.

"Let's look down there," I said, indicating the archway. "We've got to be methodical and

196

systematic, so we know we won't miss anything. OK? Remember, go carefully; we don't want to leave any sign we've been here, just in case."

The others nodded. We'd been through all this before, but the repetition of it was reassuring.

We crept into the passage, the sleeves of our coats brushing against the walls. There was another light switch at the far end. Here was a second room, larger than the first. It was lined with wooden cupboards, all of them old and hefty. Some had drawers from top to bottom and others had pull-down slatted fronts, the sort of thing you see on antique desks.

I tried a couple of drawers, and then a couple more. They were all locked.

The only way out of this room, apart from going back the way we had come, was down yet more steps, wide ones, disappearing at a steep angle into near-darkness. Standing at the edge, with Jo and Liam right behind me, I could see that the steps ended in another coded door, this one made of reinforced metal.

"Down there," I said.

"Must be a cellar," said Liam. "D'you see, it's one level down from where we came in."

"There must be something secret in there, it's got another keypad," I said. Our voices sounded weirdly deadened by the low ceiling, and by the cupboards behind us.

Keeping close together, we descended to the lower level. This second door was a dull grey, cold to the touch. The large grip it had, in place of a handle, and the seam in the wall to one side of it, showed that it slid aside rather than opened inwards. The smell down here was different, faintly queasy, like the smell you get inside a brand-new fridge.

Liam got to work exactly as before. Two minutes later, we heard the clank of a bolt pulling back. The door glided across easily, on well-oiled tracks. Beyond it was pitch dark.

I reached out and turned on the overhead lighting. It blinked into life, sharp and cool, faintly blue, and bright enough to make us shield our eyes for a few moments.

The room was starkly tiled in white, both floor and walls. There were a couple of metal trolleys, like small tables on wheels, and a couple of tall, deep glass-fronted cabinets.

The soles of our boots squeaked gently against

the clean, shiny tiles. Nervously we walked over to one of the cabinets. Arranged on shelves inside were an array of tools. There were long, stick-like objects with curling hooks at the end; some metallic trays filled with little clips; two items that looked like drills, but which were fitted with small circular discs instead of drill bits. As I looked closer, I could see that the discs were sharply serrated, like the cutting edges of a saw.

"Aren't those…" Liam stumbled over his words, "surgical instruments?"

"Yes, I think so," I breathed. "Caroline's a GP, and Byron's a trained surgeon. Maybe they collect these things."

"Nice collection," whispered Liam. "No wonder they keep it locked up."

Jo took a step back. Suddenly, she gasped. "Oh God, look under there!"

She pointed to one of the trolleys. On its lower shelf were a number of large glass jars, with chunky vacuum-sealed lids, the modern equivalent of those biological preservation jars you see in museums.

Jo retreated across the room. She clutched at the sleeve of Liam's coat. My heart drumming,

I crouched down to see into the jars.

There were eight or nine of them, all filled with a thin yellowy liquid. Floating inside the first was a human hand, with pale empty blood vessels protruding from its stump. The skin of three of its fingers had been carefully cut away. In the second were ears, piled up on top of each other.

I stood up straight, trying to catch my breath. The rest were filled with organs and flesh, some recognizable. One held a brain. The last one contained half a human head, split lengthways, its nose pressed tight against the glass, its single eye closed as peacefully as if it had been sleeping. A short continuation of its spinal column curled at the base of the jar.

"I don't like this," said Jo unsteadily.

"Christ almighty," muttered Liam. "It's like a cross between a science lab and an abattoir."

Jo had a hand pressed across her mouth.

"Are you OK?" I said.

She looked at me and nodded sharply.

Opposite the cabinets was another sliding door. This one had been left slightly open. Without further thought, I crossed the room and pulled it aside.

It was wider and heavier than the other one, and took a lot more effort to move.

The room behind it was more than three times the size of the first. The walls and floor had the same gleaming white tiles. The place smelled cold and sour. Up in the corner, a huge extractor hummed with power, indicators flicking on and off as its fans whirred into life or wound down.

There were long metal work surfaces and big stainless steel storage units. Two large rectangular washbasins were attached side by side to the wall close to the door. Taps with long paddle handles jutted out from the tiles above them. The deep inner surfaces of the basins were worn, well used, well scrubbed.

After this brief first impression, our attention was drawn to the animals, and the machines around them. My heart began to hammer.

Close by was a neat row of chrome cages, each with straw bedding and one of those upside down water feeders you see in pet shops. I thought at first that the animals inside the cages were dead, but I could hear a rasping breath coming from one of them, and the hunched back of another was rising and falling in short, shuddering movements.

Liam stepped slightly ahead of us, staring into the cages, his face slowly twisting in disgust. "What … the *hell* … is this?" he spat.

The creatures were vile. There is no other word I can use. As I felt the blood drain from my face in horror, my mind recoiled at what had been done to them, and groped in vain for explanations about why it had been done at all.

One was a cat, or had been. Its legs had been replaced with what looked like the longer, shaggier legs of a dog. Its eyes had gone, too, replaced with larger ones that were held in place on the outside of its skull with a network of wires. The eyes turned to follow me as I approached.

Another creature had the head and body of a grey rabbit. Half the fur on its back had been shaved away, and there was heavy stitching running in four haphazard lines over its pink skin. Like the cat, its legs had been replaced, but these were stubby and mechanical, powered by a battery that sat in the straw bedding. Behind the animal, flicking at the back of the cage, twitched a long, rat-like tail. Like an afterthought. Like a joke at the rabbit's expense.

"Oh my God." Jo's fingers fluttered around her face.

The most nauseating horror was held in the cage at the end of the row. It was a small pig, little more than a piglet, I think. It was surrounded by tubes, wires, and electric pumps. Nothing had been replaced, but everything had been taken apart. Its head and neck were held at the top of the cage, its limbs to one side, its body split open, internal organs spread out like exhibits, still connected by veins and sinews. All of it was pulsing with life. Like the cat, it looked directly at me, its tongue lolling.

"What the hell have they been doing down here?" cried Liam. "Why? What for?"

I tried to pull my mind back from it. To stay objective. To stay rational, or else anger and revulsion would drown me. "Experiments," I stammered. "Like … biology homework. Picked to pieces, then kept alive, just to see if it could be done."

Here, at last, in front of me, was an explanation of what I'd seen that first night. That dog in the Priory grounds had escaped and been snatched back, to become part of all this. But why…?

"I feel sick," said Jo. She staggered back. As she did

so, she brushed against a long white plastic curtain that was screening off a section of the room. The slight crumple of it against her back made her yell in fright. She whipped round, pulling the curtain aside.

Behind it there were other cages, but these ones contained humans.

There was a brain, just like the ones in the jars, but set inside a kind of metallic web. Thin metal probes punctured it all over. A couple of suspended medical drip feeds supplied it from above. Under it was a metal tray, collecting slow drips of oily liquid. Electrical connections were linked to a tablet PC, displaying graphs that danced into little mountain ranges.

The thing was living. Thinking.

A heart, held in a similar frame, twitched steadily, beating out the seconds. Plastic tubes fed into its aorta and arteries, and blood flowed around and around, aerated via a box-like device positioned behind it, a kind of artificial lung.

A head and torso lay on its back. Where the limbs had been severed, rough circles of flesh and gristle showed, a cross-section of bone at their centres. Most of the blood had been drained, leaving the flesh ghostly except for a few livid purple bruises. The chest had been split and opened up to either side, the organs pulled out and arranged around the remains of the corpse. A coil of intestines rested across the gaping hole. Sections of skin and other tissue had been delicately sliced from sides, face, shoulders. A square portion of the scalp was gone, exposing bone beneath. The remains were those of a man about ten years older than us, maybe less.

Inside a glass-fronted refrigerator were a number of packages, wrapped in plastic sheeting. I could make out what looked like kidneys, and a stomach. In one of the larger packages was a severed head, face down, hair crudely cut down to a fuzz. I couldn't tell whether it was a man or a woman.

In our state of rising terror, we took in all these horrors in no more than a few seconds. The whole place was scrubbed, and orderly. A medical playroom for the insane.

"Shit, we've got to get out of here!" cried Liam, sweat beading on his face. "We take pictures, right now, and then we get the hell out of here!"

"We haven't seen through there," I said, pointing. At the far end of the room was a wide, rectangular arch, leading to another section of the basement that was out of sight round a curve in the wall.

"I don't want to!" cried Liam. "You've been proved correct, Sam. Both of you. Congratulations. These people are sick! Now let's get out!"

"I want to go, too," shuddered Jo quietly. "But … we ought to find out all we can."

"I think you're right," I said, fighting a rising urge to throw up. "We've gone to a lot of trouble to get here. We have to finish the job."

"Well take some of the organs out of that fridge there! Nobody's going to argue with that for evidence!" Liam replied bitterly. "What, you don't want to pick that stuff up?" He wiped at his cheek with the sleeve of his coat then took a single step.

"Don't go," said Jo. "Please, stay with us. With me. Stay together. Then we know we're all safe."

Liam's expression was an agony of indecision. If we'd gone at that moment, we *would* have been safe. There were more than forty minutes left before the Greenhills got home. We could have photographed what we'd seen, and got out without leaving any noticeable trace.

But we didn't. And it's my fault. It had been my idea to break in, and if I'd backed Liam up, then I'm sure Jo would have gone along with us. I have to live with that now.

We stepped through the archway, close together, shaking but silent, our minds numb with it all.

To the left was a kind of glass booth, reaching from floor to ceiling. Beside it was one of the trolleys from the first room, stacked with pill bottles, sterile packs containing hypodermic syringes and packs of surgical dressings.

Inside the booth was a man, on a low fold-out bed strewn with heavily stained sheets. He was dead, although from the look of him, he hadn't been for very long. He was dressed in grubby blue overalls, opened at the front, and was sprawled, half on the bed and half off. His legs ended just below the knees. His feet had been replaced by mechanical grippers, one of which was smeared with blood that had leaked from a split in the join with his skin.

His eyes were rolled up, his jaw slack. Through the opening in his overalls, we could see eyes. Dozens of them, crammed in next to each other, embedded deep into the flesh of his chest. A heaving mass of eyes. Wires sprouted from reddened skin next to some of them, connecting up to a box in the top pocket of the man's overalls. His arms were held up beside his face, his fingers frozen into claws.

Jo stifled a scream with her fists. Even muffled, the sound echoed off the tiled walls. I staggered slightly, suddenly realizing I hadn't taken a breath for what seemed like days.

Opposite the booth was a second one, to the right-hand side of the archway. Inside this one, lying on a similar fold-out bed, was a girl. Half a girl. Her face was drawn and sunken, shadowed with fatigue, and her long hair hung in matted clumps.

Several of her organs had been extracted, through a long, heavily bandaged incision in her side. They were contained in separate life-supporting machines that ticked and pumped on a wide shelf above her head, all connected together by plastic blood vessels like those we'd already seen. A laptop on the shelf controlled them.

She lay very still, her eyes staring. I thought she was dead, too.

From the waist down, the two halves stitched together in an elliptical curve, her body had been replaced with that of a large, short-haired dog. At a guess, the same dog I'd seen that first night.

Hind quarters, rear legs and a tail instead of human parts. A hybrid creation, like a grotesque mermaid.

Jo sobbed, her voice quivering. "Oh my God, it's Kat Brennan. Remember? S–She … ran off. On the news. Oh my God, Kat!"

Suddenly, the girl's eyes blinked. I almost stumbled over in fright. Her mouth opened and closed, emitting only vague sounds.

Jo's trembling fingers reached out and pressed against the glass of the booth, until she realized there was nothing that any of us could do. I felt as if I was hollow, like the tiniest push would shatter me into fragments.

Liam stood beneath the archway, his face turning from one hideous scene to another and back again. He gasped, his eyes stretched wide.

"Sick … twisted … bastards," he cried, his voice cracking with emotion.

I think the shock of it all pushed me into a kind of forced detachment. I felt like I was hearing myself speak, and watching myself act. "Evidence," I said. "Liam, give me the camera from your bag."

"What?" he yelled. His voice bounced off the walls. Fear was bursting out of him as anger. "Don't be so bloody cold! We have to help this girl first! We have to get her out of this hellhole!"

"We can't," said Jo, swiping tears away from her cheeks. She tried to grab Liam's shoulders, but he shrugged her away violently. "Listen, we can't help her."

"No!" shouted Liam. "We're not abandoning her! We can't! It's not right!"

"None of this is right," I said. "Give me the camera."

"Oh, stuff your evidence! Look at her, she's alive! Are you going to walk away? Are you? I'm bloody not!"

"If we try to disconnect her from all that machinery," I quivered, "she'll probably be dead in minutes."

"And that's a life worth living she's got there, is it?" spat Liam. He stalked about, his arms flailing, frustration powering through him. "Then we should kill her. Put her out of her misery. That's what I'd want. I bet that's what she's trying to say!"

"Go on, then!" I cried. "You can do that, can you?"

He glared at me.

Then something faded in his eyes, and he slumped. "Sick in the head, sick in the head," he muttered helplessly. He dug into his bag, and handed Jo the digital SLR camera he'd brought with him. She fumbled at its settings with her trembling fingers. I took out my phone and switched it on.

"No signal down here," I said. Jo and Liam tried theirs, too.

Jo took pictures. She had to use the flash, and a very fast exposure, otherwise camera shake turned everything into a blur. After a few minutes, she handed the camera to me.

"I can't," she said. "You do it."

I continued from where she'd left off, photographing every detail of the basement, every horrible creature, every jar of preserved organs. I took pictures of the dead man in the booth. With the bitterest feelings of self-hatred, I took pictures of Kat Brennan. Jo buried her face in Liam's shoulder, while Liam stood looking drawn and grim.

We have to do this, I kept telling myself. *We have to expose this, we have to tell the world.*

I'm not sure Kat Brennan even knew we were there. Her eyes were glazed and distant. It was life in name only. Her mind had long gone. Even so, walking away from her ripped my heart from my chest.

I hurriedly stuffed the camera back into Liam's bag, and he slung it over his shoulder. We stood in the basement's first room, with the medical trolleys and the collections of instruments. I assumed that I looked every bit as pale and scared as Jo and Liam did.

This place wasn't the work of one madman, was it? Surely, the rest of the family couldn't live with it and stay silent?

Without saying another word, I switched off the lights and closed the basement's sliding entrance. As it bumped shut, we could hear the bolt snap back into place behind it.

Liam checked his watch. He spoke with forced calm, the way you hear people speak on the news, at the scene of a tragedy. "Well, no cops have turned up. You were right about no alarms, Sam."

I think we were all feeling that same kind of stunned acceptance, a numbness that insisted we had to pull ourselves together and get on with it now. My mind was still reeling. If it hadn't been, my phone wouldn't have stayed in my pocket at that moment.

We went up the stone steps, and back into the

room lined with locked drawers and cupboards. I led the way along the narrow passage, into the area behind the door that opened on to the rear garden, and from which steps ascended into the main part of the house.

I hesitated, looking up the stairs. "Do you think we should look up there?"

"We've seen enough, haven't we?" whispered Jo. "We must have seen the worst."

"Yes," I mumbled.

A muffled thud suddenly came from upstairs.

The three of us froze to the spot in terror. "What was that?" gasped Liam.

"There's someone else in the house," I breathed.

Chapter Eleven

"There can't be," whispered Jo.

"Run!" hissed Liam.

I put out a hand to stop him. "If someone's upstairs, someone else could be right out there in the garden, too, waiting."

"Cops?" said Jo.

"They'd just have come down and got us, wouldn't they?" whsipered Liam. "There's only one way into that cellar. If someone wanted to catch us, they could corner us down there far more easily. There can't be anyone waiting – that's rubbish."

"There can't be anyone at all," said Jo quietly. "They'd have heard us coming in. We made enough noise, and this back door creaked like hell."

"It wasn't footsteps," I whispered. "It sounded like something falling over."

"That's probably all it is, then," whispered Liam.

"But it must have been quite heavy," I said.

"To make a thumping sound like that. It must have been loud up there. Heavy things don't just fall over."

"What if… What if it's another of their victims?" hissed Jo. "Someone locked up? Trying to escape? We know at least one other person's gone missing in the last few weeks. Maybe they *did* hear us coming in! Maybe they can't cry out! What if they're trying to attract our attention?"

We glanced at each other, unsure what to think.

"Well, it's not the Greenhills," I muttered. "They're halfway across the Atlantic."

Our helpless revulsion at having to leave Kat Brennan was gnawing at our guts. That was what drove us on. That was what stopped us from thinking straight.

"If anyone was coming for us, they'd be here by now," said Liam. "Waiting for us doesn't make sense. It must be someone else in trouble."

Jo rubbed a shaky hand across her forehead. "You're right. It can't wait, they might be dying, or desperate. We have to look for them."

Suddenly, my mind flashed back to that face at the window, weeks before. Had it been someone looking for help? Had that eerie smile...? I felt my spine collapse like shattering glass.

Fuelled by what we thought was a fresh sense of purpose, the three of us climbed the stairs.

At the top, we emerged into a broad hallway, with a polished wooden floor and stylishly framed family photographs hanging on pastel walls. There was a curving structure above our heads, the underside of a sweeping staircase.

The floor creaked slightly underfoot. As we walked further out into the hall, we could see up the staircase. A tall stained-glass window shining wintry light on to a landing. Up above, the stairs joined a kind of balcony.

Keeping together, listening intently for further sounds, we peeked into each room we passed. None of them were locked. All were tastefully decorated, formal but comfortable. A scattering of magazines lay on the floor beside an armchair. The red standby light glowed on the TV. A corner writing desk was heaped with papers.

In the kitchen, which looked out on to the garden, pots and pans dangled from a chrome hanging rack above a rectangular island unit. A hefty,

American-style fridge hummed. A dozen handles reared up out of a wooden knife block.

A slightly smaller room at the front of the house was partly a library, partly a games room. A console was hooked up to a wall-mounted screen. Round the walls were smart white bookshelves, filled with volumes of every shape and size.

"Over there!" hissed Liam.

I hurried across the hall. Beside a grandfather clock that ticked a low, slow beat, he'd spotted another keypad.

"There's no door here, though," said Jo. "What does it operate?"

"Whatever it is, it probably leads to this other victim we heard! Quick, let's get it open."

Liam took the laptop from his bag. When the keypad activated, we heard the corresponding clunk come from inside the wall itself. A narrow section of the wall, complete with grandfather clock fixed to it, could be pushed inwards.

"What is it – a panic room?" said Jo.

"In a Georgian mansion?" I said. "Probably a pantry, or something similar, that's been disguised."

Inside, the lights came on automatically.

The room was average size, but had no window.

At first sight, it appeared to be a study. Shelves went from floor to ceiling, all the way round the room, every shelf filled to capacity with books, files, small storage boxes…

And more jars. More specimens. Old ones, this time, smaller and domed.

I realized that this must be Gottfried Hugelgrun's collection. The liquid inside these jars was dark, and brownish, the specimens themselves colourless with age. Many were unidentifiable, and those that could be identified were only recognizable by their shape.

Hands. Feet. Brains.

There was a small, low wooden table that acted as a desk, a fold-out chair propped against it. Liam picked up a dusty cardboard box and gently lifted the lid. It was filled with loose teeth. He slapped it back on to the table with a horrified cry. It rattled.

Slowly, the truth about this room dawned on us. A creeping, biting ache of horror gradually crawled up our insides.

We took a thick hardback from a shelf. On the cover, in felt tip, was '1975/6'. It was a journal, filled with handwritten notes and diagrams, cross-sections of body parts, records of experiments that obviously related to the things we'd seen in the basement. I picked out another. More of the same, but this one in a cramped, inky style. It was dated 1891 and written in German. Translations tucked into the pages referenced the work of Luigi Galvani and Allesandro Volta. On another shelf, a file of loose papers from 1906. On another, notebooks detailing the grafting of skin, bone and muscle tissue on to living people, dated 1958, 2004, 1995, 1917. A tiny, delicate volume was stamped 1888.

There were files filled with photographs pasted to sheets of paper. On the papers, more notes about experimental results. In the pictures, stuff that made the ones we'd just taken in the basement seem innocent. Pictures going back ten years, twenty, thirty, forty. There were old, ragged-edged sepia prints from the earliest days of photography.

Fat, disc-shaped cans of film. Data CDs and DVDs, old-fashioned plastic audio cassettes, even older reel-to-reel tapes, videotape cassettes, computer floppy discs from the 1980s. I unwound strips of film from their reels, saw screams and incisions caught forever.

Other documents had been filled in by the victims themselves. Horrible day-by-day log entries of how they were feeling as they were dosed with drugs, or kept alive after amputations, or hooked up to machines. The Greenhills must have made them do it. There were a couple of victims' sketchbooks, too. Agonized pencil drawings of faces, imagined landscapes, loved ones.

How many people had been locked up down there over the years? How often were there living prisoners in that basement?

Pages of notes left on the table were dated over the last few months. Some were printed out, others written in at least two – no, three – different handwriting styles. Sheets of A4 inkjet photo paper showed everything that had happened to Kat Brennan, and others, in forensic detail. Some showed the hands of an old man administering an injection. Some showed very young hands, female hands, pulling innards up through a slit in flesh. I quickly turned them all face down.

Here was the truth, then.

Yes, it *was* Byron. And it was Caroline. And it was Ken.

And it was Emma. I recognized Emma's handwriting here and there, and so did Jo.

It was all of them. Going back for more than a century! A family of maniacs. A whole dynasty of bloodthirsty monsters. Recording it all, keeping it all, revelling in it all, following some huge, twisted programme of research that we now realized we'd barely *glimpsed* in the basement.

Liam, and Jo, and I, we just gaped at it all. The sheer, unravelling scale of what had been going on, it was too big to even hold it in your head all at once. The basement was the lair of a madman, but this room, this archive, multiplied the horror of it a hundred times, a *thousand* times! Here was murder on an industrial scale. Tucked away, here, in this house, for so long.

Almost without thinking, I picked up one of the smaller, slimmer notebooks and pressed it deep into the back pocket of my jeans. "Evidence," I muttered.

We'd only spent a few minutes in the archive, but we were all conscious of the fact that we'd been wrong. The victim we'd heard wasn't to be found in here.

"We've got to search upstairs," said Liam.

Closing up the archive behind us, so that nobody could tell we'd been inside, we crossed the hall. Jo took a few steps towards the curved staircase. "Nobody's coming," she muttered. Then she called up, her voice shattering the stillness. "Hello? Hello?"

There was no reply, at first. But then…

A voice. High-pitched, a young voice, a woman's.

"Help! Is there someone there? Can you help me?"

Chapter Twelve

Without a moment's thought, all three of us raced up to the second floor. The sound of our boots pounded on the stairs.

"Where are you?" shouted Liam.

"We're in here," came the voice, from a room to our right.

"We?" I said.

Liam was the first one to enter the room. Jo and I almost collided with him, as he stopped in mid-step.

The room was very large, although there was little furniture. A TV was fixed to a wall. It showed that morning's *Daily Telegraph* on an internet feed. There was a soft, rhythmic sound of mechanical apparatus.

Two figures turned towards us. Two very old people, a man and a woman. The woman's face was narrow, but filled out with mechanical implants that gave it a lopsided shape. I realized, with utter dismay, that *hers* was the one I'd seen at the window.

The man was rounder, fleshier, but equally shrivelled and folded.

They moved towards us, their mobile life support systems carried on little wheels at the base of their frames. The movement must have been controlled directly from their brains. Short electrical connections pierced the upper parts of their heads. Neither of them moved their hands.

They weren't entirely human any more. Both were fixed in sitting positions, their backs bolt upright in steel frames that extended from their necks, round their sides to the floor. Inside the frames, machines similar to those in the basement pumped fluids and regulated organs. A set of plastic bellows functioned as the woman's lungs. The man's heart pulsed inside a glass container underneath his seat. Both of them were enmeshed in narrow tubes and electronics that weaved in and out of neatly cut holes in their smart clothes. Both the man's arms, and one of the woman's legs, had clearly belonged to someone else.

The woman drew closer to us and I noticed that her eyes didn't match each other. She had an e-reader mounted in front of her at shoulder height. As her lips moved, her voice emerged from a speaker built into her shoulder. It was the high, young voice we'd heard downstairs.

"Hello, dears. Are you friends of Emma's?" She gave us a toothy, lopsided grin.

I heard myself say, "Yes."

"I'm so glad you're here," she said. "I knocked my lady off the window sill, and I can't pick her up."

She wheeled back a little. There was a hefty, bronze figurine, a sylph in a languid pose, lying face down on the carpet by the window.

"It's a silly place to put her," said the woman, "because I'm always looking out at the park. She ought to be on the sideboard, really."

"W-Who are you?" said Jo.

"Dear me," said the man, his voice generated by a less realistic system, "we're forgetting our manners. My name is Godfrey, this is my wife Martha, and over there is my mother, Helga."

I hadn't even noticed anyone else. She was confined to a corner, where most of the mechanical sounds in the room were coming from. Helga was little more than a shell, a husk of skin and bone in the middle of a bank of externalized organs. Her brain was fixed into a glass tube that blossomed from the back of her head, and she watched us with someone else's eyes, tapping with a young but frail hand at a touchscreen beside her. She slowly nodded a greeting.

Words fell quietly from my lips, dredged up from my research. "Gottfried and Marta. Born 1902, 1903. Helga, 1877."

"Did Emma call you from the car?" said Marta. "Last-minute changes of plan are always so tedious. Are you with us for lunch? I'm afraid we don't partake ourselves these days, but it's always lovely to meet new people."

"I wasn't aware they were back from the airport yet," said Gottfried. "So disappointing about the flight being cancelled like that. You can't rely on anything today, can you?"

My blood turned to ice.

Liam seemed to crumple. He dropped to his knees, shaking his head, emitting a sound that was half laugh, half sobbing wail.

"Oh dear," said Marta. "I'm so sorry, was it something I said?"

"I think I'd better give Byron a call," said Gottfried. A dialling tone suddenly burred from his speaker, and a numeric pad flicked up on the TV screen.

"Got to get out of here," muttered Jo. "Sam, help me."

Quickly, she took hold under one of Liam's arms, and I took the other. We couldn't haul him to his feet, so we more or less dragged him out of the room and along the corridor.

"Would one of you replace my lady?" called Marta. "By the window? If you'd be so kind?"

"How rude," called Gottfried. "Young people today."

We dragged Liam out of the room and to the top of the staircase. He was shaking with semi-laughter, letting himself flop like a dead weight.

"Liam!" I shouted. "Snap out of it!"

"Liam!" cried Jo.

No response.

"We can't get him downstairs like this," I shuddered, "we'll bloody well fall and break our necks."

I scrambled in my coat for my phone.

"Do that when we get *out*!" screeched Jo. "They're coming back! We have to get *out*! Lift him!"

We tucked our heads under his arms this time, and awkwardly pulled ourselves upright.

"Liam!" yelled Jo. "Walk!"

He placed his feet flat on the floor. It was all we were going to get.

We staggered down the stairs carefully, one step at a time, terror screaming in our ears to hurry, hurry, hurry, get away, get out and run. I could feel my knees begin to shake, both with fear and with Liam's weight.

At the bottom of the staircase, we hurried for the front door. Quickest way out. We'd got about halfway there before Jo's grip on Liam slackened and he slumped down again. We were right beside the hidden archive. The concealed door was firmly shut, exactly as we'd left it.

Sounds of movement came from upstairs. Slow, mechanical.

Panic suddenly rushed through me like a flash flood. My hands shaking uncontrollably, I took a grip on Liam again. "Get up! Come on! *Come on!* They could be here any minute!" Sheer adrenaline allowed us to haul him up again. We staggered across the hall and into a darkened entrance lobby.

The front door was big and hefty, with a tall shoe rack to one side, and an antique umbrella stand to the other. I hung on to Liam while Jo scrambled with the door's two deadlocks. There were no small windows here, or lights.

"I can't see! I can't see!" wailed Jo.

Liam shook his head slowly. I heaved him upright. The deadlocks clicked uselessly as Jo fumbled. "How do you work these?" she squealed in panic. "How?"

I let Liam slide to the floor. His head rested against the shoe rack. He was still keeping up a steady stream of sobs.

Jo stood aside. I squeezed my hands into fists for a moment to help them stop trembling. I flipped the catch on the first deadlock off, then the second. I operated both at once, while Jo turned the fat, black door knob.

"Let's go!"

I flung the front door open. A rush of daylight and biting cold air hit us in the face.

The Greenhills were about to reach the front step. All four of them.

Byron Greenhill had his house keys in his hand. Caroline and Emma were right behind him. Emma's grandfather, Ken, had a rifle resting in the crook of his arm. As soon as I swung the door open, he raised it to his shoulder.

I was so shocked, there was a fraction of a second when I couldn't move. Then I turned back into the house, a yell escaping my throat. Jo screamed.

Where I was going, I have no idea. There was no way I could have got away from them.

I hadn't taken more than two or three paces before I heard a loud crack behind me. Then there was a sharp pain between my shoulder blades.

I thought – I know I specifically thought – that I was going to die. It's wrong, what they say, about your life flashing before your eyes. All that went through my head was a cry for help, selfish and bleating.

I heard Ken Greenhill's voice. "Aha! You never lose the knack! Good thing I'd left this in the boot, eh?"

I could feel a buzzing numbness rush through my limbs, a sudden loss of feeling. I couldn't tell if my feet were on the ground any more, or even if I had feet.

The polished wooden floor of the big hallway

appeared to spring up at me. It hit my arm first. I didn't feel it. My face cannoned into the sleeve of my coat. Suddenly, the world was sideways. I could see the hallway, and Jo running across it. I think she was trying to reach the steps down to the back door.

Another loud crack. She cried out. I thought the dash of red at her collar was blood, but it wasn't. It was a little dart. It stuck out of the side of her neck. She made a half-hearted grab for it, but her legs buckled beneath her and she toppled, sprawling across the floor.

"Bullseye!" Ken Greenhill shouted.

Everything went black.

Chapter Thirteen

I didn't dream. There was no sensation of time passing at all.

Everything went black in the hall and, an instant later, my mind was swimming into consciousness again. I was sitting on something cold. My stomach hurt. I could hear voices, the clatter of metal, a slight echo.

My eyes were gunged up and heavy. The first thing I saw was those tiles. The white tiles of the basement. I was on the floor, propped against a wall, my ankles tied with cord and my wrists tied behind my back. Slowly, I raised my head. I was in the main area, near the animals.

"Daddy, he's awake," said Emma.

She was standing a couple of metres from her father, on the opposite side of the room. They were sorting through trays full of medical instruments. They wore white lab coats that were patterned all over the front in a faint pink, where blood had been washed out of them over and over again. Byron turned to face me. The lab coat he was wearing looked like the one he'd worn at the Halloween party. Underneath it was a dark blue suit and silk tie. His shoes were polished to a perfect shine.

"Ah!" he said. "Jolly good."

There was a movement beside me, and I suddenly noticed that Jo was tied up on the floor, too. However, unlike me she had a gag pulled tightly round her mouth. Her eyes shone with terror, roving around the room.

"Yes, we had to gag her," said Byron, who had turned towards me. "I couldn't stand the hysterics. *You're* not going to make a fuss, now, are you, Sam?"

I just stared at him. "Why?" I said at last.

"What's that? Speak up, young man."

"Why?" I said loudly. "Why are you doing this?"

Byron tut-tutted, like a teacher answering a stupid question. "You've got a whole file full of research, which we'll have to confiscate later, and now you've also had a good snoop around our home. I would have thought the answer was obvious."

"You'd better not have gone into my room,"

muttered Emma, busy at the metal worktop.

I talked to occupy my mind, to stop myself from collapsing into despair. "Is all this to keep members of your family alive? Those mobile corpses upstairs? Transplants? Life support systems?"

Byron snorted. "You're disappointing me, Sam. Emma said you were a bright boy. Of course, naturally we do want to keep our loved ones with us, although in the case of a blustering old windbag like Grandpa Godfrey it's not always clear why."

Emma laughed.

"It's far more than that," said Byron. "We're seeking, if you like, the holy grail of medicine. We're working towards a fundamental understanding of the human condition, the human body, so that we can transcend nature, so that we can triumph over it and cheat death forever."

"Eternal life?" I breathed.

"I can hear the scepticism in your voice," grinned Byron, his fleshy jaw spreading. "Good for you, there's a spark of intelligence after all. It's very early days, yet. We've barely begun our work."

"Over a hundred years?" I spat. Fear was clouding my judgement again, making me angry and gobby.

"You can't be very good at it."

"Oh, nonsense, we've made enormous progress, but we're dependent on so many aspects of technology," said Byron. "Plus, of course, we're forced to do our valuable work in secret."

"That's a shame for you, huh?" I raged bitterly.

"Yes, it is," said Byron, without any hint of irony. "Are you ready, Emma?"

She dropped a scalpel into a tray, then spun on her heels and saluted. "Aye aye, cap'n."

"Wheel him in, then."

She vanished for a moment, then returned pushing one of the large metal trolleys ahead of her. She positioned it in the middle of the room, and locked its wheels with the toe of her trainer. From the angle I was at, I didn't have a clear view of what was on the trolley, but poking-up feet and a shock of hair was enough to tell me that it was Liam.

"What are you going to do to him?" I cried.

Byron tutted again. "I'm not even going to answer that one," he muttered.

"He's a playground," said Emma brightly, excitement dancing in her eyes. "Practice makes perfect. At the moment, I'm learning how much of the human body can be cut away before vital functions cease. You'd be amazed. You can remove a *lot* of stuff."

"Learning?" I gasped.

"Of course, learning," said Byron, checking through the instruments on the worktop. "Emma is of an age, now, when her training is well under way. She's worked her way up from simple projects to more advanced techniques. Eventually she'll take over the running of the family firm, just as I took over from my father, and he took over from his father before him, that lovable old windbag."

"The recent murders," I said. "The missing people, the deaths. They were part of your training?"

"Yup," said Emma. "There's lots to learn. I mistimed the man in the park. I had to leave the body or I'd have been seen by that dog walker. The training period is a thrilling time for the family. You know, a tradition, one generation handing over to the next."

"A baptism, if you will," said Byron. "A short, concentrated spate of projects to kick off a new member of the clan. She's already very good indeed at covering her tracks. The park incident aside, that is. Even so, she's better than I was at her age. I made the odd mistake twenty-odd years ago, I can tell you. Did you see the report last week about the man in the rat-infested house? That was all her idea."

She smiled. "Thank you, Daddy."

"Credit where credit's due, darling," said Byron. "Take a box of young rats with you, then let them loose when you've harvested the organs you want, and there's a ready-made story for the press and Mr Plod the policeman. Simple, and effective. You've even got a box ready to take your stuff home with you. Why didn't we think of that one before?"

Behind my back, I pulled and twisted at the thin cord that was tied round my wrists. My hands and arms were sweating so profusely that I was gradually loosening its grip. It pinched my skin painfully, but I was beginning to shift it a little further towards my fingers.

"The trick is," said Emma, her expression alive with glee as she looked at me, "to mix and match your methods. Bodies sliced up in the park are a thrill, but more than a couple are too much to hush up completely. You need to fit the story to the

237

person. So, you make kids involved in gangs look like they've run away, or dads look like they've deserted their families, or mums apparently die of unexpected complications at the hospital, blah blah blah. Just snatching lost souls off the street, that's the ideal scenario, the easiest, but it takes a while to identify one. Sometimes you just have to settle for a drunk or a squatter. We choose carefully. We would never take anyone who's worth anything."

I tried desperately to think of something that might stall them. "People know we're here," I cried. "We told people we were coming here today. You'd better get out, they'll be here soon. We told them."

"No, you didn't," said Byron casually, without so much as glancing up from the surgical instruments he was checking. "However, the three of you have made quite a mess for us to clear up, haven't you. Your parents are already under my wife's care, so that won't be an issue, but explaining the absence of the other two will take some careful thought. Any ideas on that score yet, darling?"

"No, not really," said Emma.

"Well, I'll leave it in your capable hands."

Emma suddenly perked up, as if something had

occurred to her. "You know, I've never had a personal connection with a specimen before. And now, here are three all at once. It's going to be facinating."

"Yes," said Byron, "it's very unusual. We did have to deal with an accountant about ten years ago, who'd been overcharging your mother. She had a whale of a time with him. You were only little, darling, you probably won't remember."

"I do, I was six," said Emma. "Was he the one we put the extra legs on?"

"That's right, well done. Honestly, the look on his face. It still makes me laugh."

By now, Emma was placing broad straps across the trolley, holding Liam tightly in place at his head, chest, waist and feet. Byron was cutting at Liam's hair with a large pair of scissors.

I fought back the feeling of hopelessness that was beginning to drown me. I had to keep talking, delay them starting work on Liam, do something, give myself time to think of a way out, a way to save us.

"You're wrong," I cried. "We've left notes at home, all of us, saying where we've gone."

"No, you haven't," drawled Byron. "Although, as I say, clearing up will pose a challenge. We may need to create the odd item of evidence, or have a word in an ear or two. Inconvenient, but can't be helped, I suppose."

The cords tying my wrists behind my back were definitely looser. Not by much, but maybe enough. I had to keep them talking, distract them as best I could.

"But," I said, "you surely don't just kill a few people once a generation. That can't account for what we saw in that sick archive of yours. What about the rest of the time?"

"Oh yes," said Byron, "we take specimens fairly regularly, as we need things. Or as the mood takes us, I suppose. Sometimes, one simply fancies a rummage around."

"It's insane, how can you not be found out?" I cried.

Byron sighed. "As Emma has already explained, young man, more than one or two bodies in one place looks peculiar, but many bodies spread across the whole country, or other countries... Well, that's just life, isn't it? When we need something, we normally take a long drive."

"How the hell can you bring bits of people back

240

from abroad?" I cried. "How can people not notice the deaths?"

"Think, boy," said Byron. "With my credentials and connections, do you actually believe that I can't send back vital scientific research materials from overseas? And as for murders, these things are commonplace. Do you have any idea how many people are reported missing in this country? Hmm? There were over 300,000 in 2012 alone. That's a fact. Nearly all of them are accounted for, in one way or another, but about two per cent stay missing. Around six thousand. And can you guess how many unidentified body parts were found in that same year? No? Nearly ninety. Ninety different people, chopped up but unaccounted for. People don't notice, and don't care."

"Are you trying to tell me you experiment on six thousand people a year?"

Byron laughed. "For goodness' sake, of course not! We do have *lives* outside work, you know! The government takes quite a few, for their own purposes, various companies take some, on licence, assorted oddballs and perverts soak up most of the remainder. There are relatively few scientific studies

241

like ours. I'd estimate we account for … ooh, around a dozen or so, on average. It'll come to rather more than that this year, of course."

"That can't be true," I scoffed. "It's *impossible*."

"I'll just get the bone saws, Daddy," said Emma. She left the room again.

Byron called after her. "They're in the top drawer, don't forget!" There was no answer.

"You're all insane," I babbled. "Out of your minds."

He stared at me for a moment, his round eyes turning my flesh cold. He put down the scissors and walked round the trolley to stand over me. His perfect shoes clacked on the white tiles. The hems of his dark blue trousers hung exactly level.

"There's something that people like you never seem to appreciate," he said, "and that's the fact that people like me and my family have a right to do what we do."

"What?"

He crouched down beside me. I could smell a woody cologne on him.

"The underclass are simply resources," he said. "That's what they're for. The hoi polloi, the 'Great

242

Unwashed' as Bulwer-Lytton put it. The poorest, the struggling and the needy. We shepherd them. We, the select few, must direct them as we see fit. That is how it has always been, throughout human history, and that is how it will always be. Show me one society, one nation, anywhere on this earth where money and power is not concentrated in the hands of the elite. It's the natural order. A few politicians have tried to turn things on their head over the centuries – Russia, China, for example – and look what a disaster that's always turned out to be."

"Your kind of insanity is a disaster, too," I said. The cords behind me were almost over my knuckles. My hands were almost free.

"Dear me, have you learned nothing?" said Byron in a tone heavy with condescension. "For all except the few, freedom is an illusion, just like its silly friend 'democracy'. These things are inventions to pacify the masses. You're free to choose! Free to vote! It's a nonsense. You're free to choose only what you can afford. What you do, how you spend your time, where you go, everything depends on how much *money* someone else will give you, in exchange for the ticking clock of your short life. The average yokel's only choice is between one form of imprisonment and another. Money is the only freedom, power is the only politics. The masses can't be given decisions to make, or problems to solve – there'd be chaos. They're not qualified for the job. Economies and governments may rise and fall, Sam, but the richest remain rich and the poorest remain poor, and everyone else fights to the death for cash and status. Only the properly educated and responsible can lead. The rest must do as they're told, whether they realize it or not, otherwise our civilization will simply crumble."

"I've never heard such shit in all my life!" I spat.

Byron spread his hands. "There you are, you're making my point for me. Faced with an opinion you don't share, you resort to coarse language. You come from an impoverished background, Sam, and it shows. You people want fairness, justice and equality? You can't even look after yourselves. You eat junk, you think junk, you watch junk, you're vulgar and you're lazy. If one of you people was given a garden to tend, all you'd do is dump a fridge in it! The function of your sort is to consume, and to work, to keep the wheels turning for the benefit of your betters. It's as simple as that."

"The poor can still have morals," I said. "Something you clearly don't have. I think that's worth more than money!"

Byron shrugged. "We as a family more than compensate society for those we utilize, through our extensive charity. That's fair, isn't it? Morality is a very old-fashioned idea. In today's world of commerce and progress, it's becoming steadily less relevant. Are you really telling me that the life of a work-shy benefits scrounger on a rundown estate is worth exactly the same as the life of, say, a great engineer or a medical consultant, someone who improves the lives of others, and pays their taxes?"

"Yes."

He stood up straight, chuckling to himself, and walked back around to the other side of the trolley on which Liam was strapped.

"I'm sure you're simply saying that for effect, young man. If you had both those individuals hanging from the edge of a cliff, you know perfectly well which one should be saved first. What if it was a rapist and Mozart hanging there instead, eh?"

"I'd let you drop, that's for sure," I growled.

As I spoke, one of my hands came free! I kept them as still as possible. Now I had to untie the cords round my ankles without either Byron or Emma noticing. Where had Emma got to?

Byron was warming to his theme. "The value of an individual is directly correlated to his or her education, job, disposable resources and so on, but society's bleeding hearts stubbornly refuse to face the truth, and as a result we're forced to work down here in secret instead of in a fully staffed laboratory."

"So, you drug people into docility when you need them not to notice things, and to protect yourselves you maintain a network of powerful friends. Friends who are ignorant of the full truth, I assume?"

"Mostly," said Byron, in a matter-of-fact tone. "The drugs are a personal fascination, as you can imagine. The pharmacological mixes required for our few regular patients makes an interesting hobby, although I've never been able to eliminate the occasional side effect. They almost all get a runny nose; it's quite puzzling."

At that moment, Emma returned carrying two of the serrated silver drills we'd seen earlier.

Electrical cables were wound round them.

"They were in the top drawer," she said, slightly out of breath.

"I did call after you," said Byron.

"While I was searching, I had more time to think about cover stories for Liam and Jo," said Emma, "and I'm thinking that there needs to be an Elton Gardens link, but I still can't come up with a plausible one."

"Not to worry," said Byron, taking the bone saws from her and unwinding the cables. "We've got a day or two yet."

"That's a resource, too, isn't it," I breathed. "Ken Greenhill had the whole estate built in the first place. You keep it as a ready-made human dump, for taking victims and hiding crimes."

Emma gawped at me. "Well, dur!" she exclaimed. "Why else would a place like that be found in a town like Hadlington? We don't have to do much to keep it a dump – the people who live there manage that for themselves. It makes things much easier for the police, too. It gives them a terrifically high clear-up rate."

"Especially with your uncle as chief constable," I said. Facts from my research swam back into my mind. "Ken had that path built, too. You've even got your own back-door route down to the estate."

"Exactly," said Emma.

The wave of hopelessness was beginning to swamp me all over again. I held my wrists together, trying to push aside the fear that was clouding my head. *Keep them talking*, I thought. *Let me think.*

"I don't care what you say," I cried, my voice unsteady. "You won't get away with this. You won't!"

Byron chuckled. He plugged the larger of the bone saws into a wall socket. "We already have," he said. "I've really enjoyed our chat, young man. Nothing like a spirited debate to stir the mind, eh? But now it's time to get down to work, so do please keep quiet for a while."

I let my mouth run on automatic. I didn't even know what I was saying. "How can you be like this? How can you enjoy it? How can you get a kick out of cutting people up? Turning them into monsters?"

Byron paused, the bone saw held to the front of his lab coat. I suddenly realized why his gaze was so unnerving, so creepy: he barely blinked. "You obviously haven't tried it."

"Don't be such a stick-in-the-mud, Sam," said Emma. "Daddy's right, you'd change your mind if you held a living brain in your hands. It's amazing. Break a piece of that brain off, hold that squishy tissue in your palm, and think of what it represents. Is this little piece of brain that person's memories? Is this their ability to ride a bike, or write a poem, or fall in love? Life is right there, in your fingers."

"But you're sick, can't you see that?" I wailed. "What kind of a person would make those horrible mixed-up animals? What diseased mind would do what you've done to Kat Brennan?"

Perhaps I'd given my thoughts enough time to clarify, or perhaps it was a moment of inspiration, but at that moment I saw I could untie myself without being observed. The trolley, with Liam lying on top of it, was quite close to me. The view that Emma and her father had of me was of my head and shoulders only. If I was careful, I could move my hands around and get at the knotted cords.

"Aren't you impressed by our work on Miss Brennan?" said Byron. He clicked the switch at the wall socket. "Human-animal hybrids are a new line of research for us. We've achieved remarkable results in only a few months. There are two areas of interest: first, the use of animal tissue, which is quicker to reproduce, as a short-term substitute for human organs; second, the genetic recoding of human tissue with animal DNA, to give us enhanced organs, with longer periods of use and greater biochemical efficiency. It's this second area that's the most exciting. A cross-species splice of chromosomes has shown us vastly improved rates of cellular growth."

"Daddy," admonished Emma. "Stop lecturing, it's such a bore."

"Sorry, darling," smiled Byron.

"And it's my turn," she said, pointing to the electric saw.

"So it is," he said. He handed her back the bone saw. She turned it on and it instantly buzzed into life, emitting a high-pitched whine as its blade spun.

I pulled at the knots behind my ankles. My fingers scratched and dug at the cords.

Emma stepped carefully towards the trolley, looking Liam up and down. The saw hissed in her hands.

"Rib cage or skull to begin with?" called Byron above the noise.

"I can't decide," said Emma. "He shouldn't kick

much either way, should he?"

"No, no, he's well under," said Byron.

The cords began to unravel. I glanced across to Jo. She was silent, curled up. Her gaze wandered around the room, terrified but distant, as if she was watching events unfold a million miles away.

Emma turned herself ninety degrees, to bring the saw into line with Liam's head. The pair of them had their attention fully focused on him. It would still be a few seconds before I could get my ankles free. I had to distract them!

"How did you get here?" I shouted. "So fast?"

Emma switched off the bone saw. "Sorry, what?"

"When you caught us?" I cried. "Why weren't you over the Atlantic?" I knew the answer, of course, but I hoped that they wouldn't realize that.

Emma and her father glanced at each other, half annoyed at me and half amused.

"If you must know," said Emma, "the plane had 'technical difficulties'. All the other flights were full until late evening, so we just threw in the towel and came home. It was quite a shock when we got a call from Grandpa Godfrey saying we had visitors."

"Yes, we're going to have to beef up security

251

now," said Byron testily. "Father's said before that we've let it slide, what with that dog getting out the other week, so he'll be crowing unbearably tonight. Absolute nuisance, you three. Now, please be quiet."

I pulled the last of the cords away. I was free.

Emma restarted the bone saw.

Chapter Fourteen

What else could I do? I asked myself then, and I ask myself even now, what choice did I have? I tell myself that there was only one thing I could do, and yet my every last atom still shrivels and burns with guilt.

I felt shaky and unsteady, but I was no longer tied up. I had to act! I had to escape. Giving in was no option.

I had to, hadn't I? It was my duty. I had to raise the alarm. I had to tell the outside world what was happening here. That much was clear. Absolutely clear. So what else could I do, except save my own skin?

Leaving my friends to their fate.

I still feel so ashamed. I can't help it.

I'd taken them into that place. The worst mistake of my life. And now I would pay for that mistake, with their blood and my eternal guilt. I have no right to ask for forgiveness. I deserve none.

There was no way I could untie Jo without being seen, let alone remove the straps holding Liam to the trolley. Jo seemed completely out of it, I assumed through shock. I couldn't pick her up and carry her, I'd never be able to move fast enough. It was highly unlikely that I'd be able to physically overpower Emma and her father, not only because there were two of them and one of me, but also because Emma, at least, was armed with a weapon I had no doubt she'd use. There was the question of them calling for assistance, too. I had no idea where Caroline and Ken were. I couldn't cut the power to the basement – I didn't know how; I couldn't stab them with their own scalpels – every instrument was within their reach and not mine; I couldn't crush them beneath the upturned trolley – in my terrified state, my strength was doubtful and the bone saw could be at my throat in a moment. There was no move I could make that they couldn't block or counter with another.

My only hope of escape, the only advantage I had, was in surprise. The one thing it was within my power to do was to run, immediately, as fast as I could, and find help.

Leaving my friends.

All these thoughts crammed through my head in the single second it took for Emma to bend over Liam, the bone saw buzzing in her hands.

Byron had said they'd have to improve their security, which implied there might be loopholes. The locks on the front door had been nothing special, firmly secure from the outside but operable from the inside.

Everything was designed to stop someone getting *in*. They must have been so sure of themselves that they hadn't paid the same attention to the possibility of someone getting *out*.

I gambled that their arrogance was their weakness. Byron had already said that the dog I'd seen had escaped from them, albeit temporarily. It must have happened while the Greenhills were dealing with whoever had made that terrible scream, the one that woke me up. Perhaps a door had accidentally been left ajar when the Greenhills descended to the basement, or perhaps a window had been open. Perhaps they'd let the dog have the run of the house anyway.

It flashed through my head. All I had to do was stand up, run into the basement's first room, up the stairs, along the narrow corridor, to the back door. I knew the way. If I couldn't open the back door, up the other stairs into the main house, across the hallway, to the front.

The bone saw was lowered over Liam's forehead.

I jumped to my feet, the cords that had bound my ankles clasped in my hand. Lashing out wildly, I whipped the cords against the bone saw. It was almost knocked from Emma's hands.

The pair of them were so surprised, they took a second to react. By the time Emma thrust the saw towards me, I was a few centimetres beyond her reach. Byron, fury twisting his face, charged around the trolley to block my path.

I was too quick for him. His outstretched fingers slid against my coat, but I was ahead of him.

I pelted across the basement and up the stairs. A bellow of rage followed me, stabbed at my pounding heart, quickened my pace. At the top of the stairs I turned and rushed along the corridor. I could see the back door. Light was spilling along the stairs that led up into the house.

I dared not look back.

I was at the back door when a fist suddenly

pounded into my back, level with my kidney. I howled with pain. A hand took hold of my hair, sharply pulling my head back.

Caroline Greenhill's face was beside mine, her eyes ablaze. "Nice try," she hissed, through gritted teeth.

The cords from my ankles were still in my hand. I slashed them across her face. She leaped back with a screech, releasing her grip on me, a thin line of blood welling on her cheek.

"You little *shit*!"

My fingers trembling, I gripped the bolts on the door and heaved. They snapped back and I flung the door open.

It was night. The freezing air tore into my face and hands.

I raced out on to the grass and only then did I look back.

Caroline was in the doorway, on her knees, her hands at her cheek. Emma was behind her, with her arms round her mother's shoulders. Behind Emma, barely visible in the shadows, stood Byron.

Emma's voice chased after me, cutting through the darkness, fiery with glee. "You belong to us, Sam Hunter!"

I almost stumbled, my heart was racing faster than my feet. Then I heard the back door slam.

How the hell I got over those tall garden railings, I don't know. Adrenaline launched me at them, and with my legs scrambling I clambered to the top. I fell off the other side, landing awkwardly on my back. The place where Caroline had punched me was throbbing with pain.

Gasping, I got to my feet and ran across the grass. Lights were on in all three of the houses in Priory Mews.

As I ran, I searched in my coat pockets. My keys were gone, and so was my phone. The Greenhills must have taken them. Disposed of with other victims' possessions. No doubt all the photos I'd taken had gone the same way.

However, they'd missed the little notebook, from their archive, that I'd tucked deep into the back pocket of my jeans. It was small, and slim, it made no bulge. Phone and keys they'd expected and looked for, the camera, too, but not this notebook. We'd closed the archive up behind us and left it undisturbed; they might not have realized we'd even been inside it. I pulled the notebook out, and turned it over in my hands a couple of times. It had bent where I'd sat on it, but was intact. I returned it to its hiding place.

I hammered at my front door. "It's me! Let me in! Quick!"

I kept looking back, past the glow of the street lamps, into the dark, watching for movement. What were they doing?

"Hey!" I hammered louder. At last, I could see Dad's shape through the frosted glass, plodding along the hall.

"Hello," he said cheerily. "Where've you been all day, then? We were trying to call you."

I pushed past him and rushed into the kitchen. I snatched up the phone, and took it into the living room. As the dial tone burred in my ear, I looked out of the window at the street.

"Are you all right, Sam?" said Mum. She was watching TV. "Could you not stand there? You're in my way."

Nothing out the front.

I returned to the kitchen, switched off the light, stared out across the back garden. Everything was dark and still.

Mum and Dad appeared and switched the light back on.

"Have you got your school project done, then?" said Dad. "Where in town did you go?"

"You've been such a long while, we were starting to get worried," said Mum. "Is everything all right?"

"No, everything's not all right," I said.

They smiled their drugged smiles at me. What cocktail of medications was running through their veins, I wondered. I wanted to yell at them, but I could see it would be a wasted effort.

My hands were shaking as I held the phone.

I was about to dial 999, when a cold sensation of doubt suddenly stopped me.

Emma's uncle was chief constable, for God's sake. Also, I knew from the Halloween Ball that at least one of Leonard Greenhill's colleagues was drugged. If I called the police here in Hadlington, would someone make sure that my story was ignored? Would the Greenhills' influence turn me into a malicious liar?

No, I had evidence, right there in my pocket.

Evidence that I'd have to hand over, if I was going to be believed. Evidence that could be quietly returned to its owners.

Was *that* why the Greenhills weren't chasing after me?

I'd have to be silenced, wouldn't I? What if the police turned up, here, right now, summoned by the Greenhills? What if the police found something illegal planted in my room? What if I'd walked into a trap?

What if I couldn't even trust Mum and Dad? How far under the Greenhills' control were they?

My trembling finger stayed poised over the phone.

"Are you hungry?" said Mum. "Did you have something to eat in town? There's some lasagne left if you want it."

"No, I had that," said Dad.

"Have any of the Greenhills been here today?" I said, raising my voice to get their attention. "Please, this is very important."

"No, why?" said Dad.

"Or anybody else, at all?" I said.

"Nope," said Dad.

"How are you getting on with Emma?" smiled Mum.

I screwed up my eyes. Think think think! They knew I was out in the open, but they didn't know

I'd got proof with me. What would they expect me to do? How would they make sure I was got out of the way?

"I'm a sitting duck here," I muttered. "Why the hell didn't I just run the other way? It would be the easiest thing in the world for them to frame me. They wouldn't have to go anywhere near anything suspicious. Christ, they could even murder you two and make it look as if I'd done it! I've got to leave. Or would that look as if I'm on the run?"

"I think someone's had a tiring day," said Mum. "I'll do you some beans on toast."

"Shut up!" I snapped. "I'm trying to think!"

Mum folded her arms. "There's no need for rudeness," she said quietly.

I had to get a message out to somewhere safe, and quickly. That was it!

I knew who to call, but the phone sat uselessly in my hand.

"I can't remember the number!" I wailed. "It's in mine, it's not on this one!"

"Which number?" asked Dad.

"Jo's dad," I cried. Saying her name sent a dagger through my head.

"That's why we were trying to call you!" said Dad.

"W–What?" I said.

"Trying to call you," repeated Mum. "Yes, Jo's mum rang a bit before teatime. She was trying to find out where Jo had got to. She was awfully upset, poor thing."

I felt the blood grow cold in my veins. "Why?"

"It's her dad. He died this afternoon. Everyone thought he was on the mend, and some doctor came to visit him, and he had a clean bill of health."

"Half an hour later, another heart attack," said Dad. "Just goes to show. Could happen to anyone."

"He was a bit fat, apparently," said Mum. "You should take that as a warning and go on a diet, Richard. You're asking for trouble."

Without a word, I dropped the phone on to the kitchen table. Who to trust? What to do? Fight-or-flight.

I had to get out, while it was still possible, before the Greenhills' plan, whatever it might be, could trap me.

"Have you got some money?" I said.

"There's plenty in my wallet if you want it," said Dad.

"I'll … see you later, OK?"

263

"Are you going out again?" said Mum. "Thank goodness it's not a school night."

I scooped the wallet off the hall table, removed a handful of notes, and left the house. Outside, I kept well away from the glow of the street lights.

Looking back, the Priory stood, huge and silent, lurking in the dark. A few lights were visible behind curtained windows. The Renault stood in the drive. Normality. A family home. A house on a street in a town. Hiding secret things.

I had no sense that I was even being watched. It was as if they'd simply looked away, so confident that I wouldn't be able to expose them that they needn't give it another thought.

Whatever they had planned for me, it was going to be terrible, and final.

Someone was going to be coming for me, I thought. Someone, something, somehow. They had a fate in store for me, and I knew in my bones that it had already been set in motion.

I ran.

I would not give in, I would not give up. I would make my evidence public. They would pay for all they'd done.

My mind was so tangled, I barely knew what direction I took. I ran out on to Maybrick Road, then down the long path to the river. By the time I reached the riverbank, my lungs burned with the cold air. Clouds of breath fogged around me. A single lamp, the one I had seen Emma and her grandfather pass, cast a patch of yellow light across the black surface of the river.

The water rumbled and swirled, like a restless beast in its pit. Slender trees grew at the river's edge, their trunks pushed and bent by the ceaseless flow.

I paused to catch my breath, then ran out on to the green metal footbridge. It clanked beneath me. The Arvan rumbled and roared, the glow from the lamp stretching my shadow into a long, dissolving smear against the night.

I ran down streets, into the middle of Elton Gardens. I wasn't aware of having any destination, my thoughts were too confused, but I guess now that I was cutting across the estate to make for the town centre and the newspaper's offices.

A few minutes later I arrived at the parade of shops that stood on one of the two main roads running through the estate. A couple of them were boarded up, the plywood covering their windows scrawled with graffiti. There was also a small hair salon, a chemist's and a newsagent's, all closed for the night with shutters down. An off-licence and a chip shop at the end of the row were the only shops open. I sat on one of a line of broken wooden benches, cemented into the paving slabs outside the chippie.

'Elton Gardens Fish Saloon'. There was a short queue at the high counter. A skinny woman in yellow Chinos was placing her order. An Asian man was tipping a bucket of chopped potatoes into the fryer. The clock on the wall above the counter showed it was just gone ten past nine.

I sat gathering my thoughts, my face in my hands, staring at the distorted reflections from the shops on the damp pavement. My muscles ached from running. I felt exhausted, defeated, drowned.

People came and went around me. I thought maybe I should just tell someone, or show the notebook to anyone passing by.

How many of them would have listened? How many would have given me strange looks and dismissive sneers? How many were spies for the Greenhills? How many would have tapped their phones and called the cops and a psychiatric ward? How long would I have lasted? I'd have been like that guy at the end of *Invasion of the Body Snatchers*, raving and shouting, a madman with a message that nobody wanted to hear. An old film I'd seen the other week, with Liam and Jo. Part of our shared nerdiness.

My heart sank at the thought of Liam and Jo.

There was no saving them, was there?

There was only vengeance. That would drive me on.

The *Hadlington Courier* was no good. The tentacles of the Greenhills were tightly squeezed around everything in town. I'd have to go much further afield. I had to talk to someone well away from any possibility of Greenhill influence, someone rational and impartial, who had enough influence of their own to ensure that the truth would be revealed.

I checked the money I'd brought with me. There was more than enough cash for a one-way ticket to London.

The railway station was about a fifteen-minute walk away. Trains into London ran until at least ten o'clock. Once I got there, I could lose myself, no problem. I could get a phone, and let Mum and Dad know I was OK. And check they were OK. Even if Mum and Dad were totally under the Greenhills' chemical spell and told them I'd called, they still wouldn't be able to track me down.

There were risks. The Greenhills might threaten my parents. But as soon as the lid was blown, as soon as the truth was out...

Decision made, I headed for the station at a brisk pace. I seemed to have found fresh energy.

Hadlington station was quiet at that time of night. There were staff milling about beside the ticket booth and a couple of taxi drivers chatted around mugs of tea in the car park.

I bought a ticket at the machine and waited on the platform, keeping to the few shadows and watching the arrivals board tick away the minutes. A bald man appeared, wearing a long overcoat and scarf, and took up a position close to the platform's edge. He stood still, looking directly ahead, except for one brief scan left and right. He saw me and kept an expression of indifference on his face. The smooth dome of his head reflected the overhead lights.

Moments later, a woman appeared, too. She also stood close to the platform edge, about ten metres along from the bald man. She had long, blond hair, a short jacket and high heels. She looked at me, too. Her expression was identical to the man's.

The 21:47 to London Marylebone rumbled into view and slowed to a halt in a hissing screech of brakes. I hurried over to the nearest carriage and hopped on board. There weren't many passengers.

Neither the man nor the woman made a move until I did. They walked along the platform and got into the same carriage as me.

I found a seat by a window, one of an empty four round a table. The doors slid shut, and there was a rising hum of power as the train moved off.

Chapter Fifteen

The bald man sat on the other side of the central aisle, directly opposite me. The woman was behind me; I couldn't see exactly where without standing up and turning around.

The train clattered and rumbled. The lights of Hadlington were left behind, and we travelled through countryside, little of it visible in the cloud-shrouded night. The bright streak of a motorway ran alongside for a short distance, then glided away behind hills.

The bald man plucked a phone from the top pocket of his overcoat. He glanced over, and caught me watching him. I turned my head, and watched his reflection in the window beside me instead. He tapped out a message, then pocketed the phone. He sat still and quiet, not even bothering to look out into the gloom. He didn't use his phone again, or take out a book, or otherwise occupy himself in any way.

I began to get nervous. Something about him didn't seem quite right. Was he just a late-night commuter? Why was he just sitting there? People don't just sit there on trains. If they've nothing to do then they doze, or at least they look bored and restless.

But, then, I was just sitting there, too. Maybe I was the one who seemed odd. Furtive. Watchful.

Or maybe I was right to be paranoid. Had he texted the Greenhills? Or someone acting on their behalf? The police?

What was the woman doing? There were barely more than a dozen passengers in this carriage – why had she sat behind me? Were they working together, making sure I was between them?

Who were they? Who the hell were they?

I tried to stay calm and focused. There were other people here; there was nothing these two could do to me out in public like this. I told myself that I was letting my imagination run away with me. I had no reason to suspect them. The Greenhills couldn't even have known that I'd go to the station, could they?

There were two stops between Hadlington and London. As the train slowly drew into the first of them, the woman suddenly appeared from behind me and stood beside the door.

Nobody got on or off, the woman included. When the train began to move again, she went back to her seat. The bald man sent a second message.

What was that about? Had she done that in case I'd tried to leave the train? Was he sending an update?

The train rattled on. A uniformed attendant plodded down the aisle, clipping tickets and sniffing. A couple further down the carriage started laughing at a private joke.

Shortly before the train was due to make its second stop, I thought of a way to test my suspicions. I stood up, walked along to a point beyond the laughing couple, and found another seat. If the man and the woman were supposed to be keeping a close eye on me, then one or the other of them would have to change seats as well. I was out of their sight.

With my heart thumping, I shifted slightly to look back along the aisle. I couldn't see the bald man any more, but the woman's high heels were poking out. I waited, watching the aisle, not shifting my gaze for a second.

The train began to slow down. The glow of the

next station suddenly flowed along the sides of the carriage. The woman got to her feet and stood beside the door again. The doors slid back, letting a bank of cold air ripple along the aisle. The woman got off and marched away, following signs saying 'Buses' and 'Platforms 2,3,4'.

Instead of feeling relieved that I'd obviously been wrong, my churning fears made me wonder if she'd left the train because her part of my surveillance was over. No more stops before London, no more opportunities for me to get off. I could tell how nervous I was because I could have sworn I heard the next-stop station announcement as 'Maybrick High'.

What about the bald man? Was he still sitting there?

The train sped up once more. I considered returning to my original seat, purely to check on the man's whereabouts. However, before I could move I saw him coming towards me. My nerves froze. He walked slowly between the seats, and stopped when he was level with the exits. Digging his hands into the pockets of his overcoat, he leaned against one of the transparent partitions beside the doors. He stood there, his weight shifted to one side, his features still set in that casual mask of disinterest.

He didn't look in my direction. Or, at least, I didn't notice if he did. I monitored him closely for the remainder of the journey, slightly less than ten minutes. He barely moved a muscle.

The train pulled into Marylebone at 22:27, exactly on time. The bald man stepped out as soon as the doors opened and I lost sight of him. I went through the ticket barriers, across the draughty concourse, out on to the road. Black cabs growled along, picking up and dropping off fares. A couple of taxi drivers chatted around mugs of tea.

My first thought was that it should be safe to contact the police here, but caution made me change my mind. I might be able to present my evidence to cops in London, but I had no guarantee that I wouldn't be dealing with one of Chief Constable Greenhill's colleagues. In any case, my claims would inevitably be handed over to the police in Hadlington at some point, and then I'd be back to square one.

For similar reasons, I dismissed the idea of contacting any official authority. There were relatives of the Greenhills in the Home Office, and elsewhere. I couldn't be sure who was a potential friend or a potential enemy. I was not going to take unnecessary chances.

The media, in some form or other, seemed like the best option. *The national papers will hear me out*, I thought. But anything I say could be dismissed, or even discredited completely if the Greenhills were able to put pressure on the right people. Something with a significant internet readership might be a safer bet, or a TV news channel.

What was clear was that simply calling them would be pointless. They'd never listen, they'd assume I was a nutter. I had to be there in person, show them the notebook.

There was a large, busy café on the other side of the street, opposite the station entrance, next to a chip shop where I could see an Asian man was tipping a bucket of chopped potatoes into the fryer. Hand-painted lettering on the café window said 'Free Wi-Fi' and 'Internet Access Here'. I dodged a line of taxis and crossed the road.

The café was warm and bustling. There was a short queue at the bar. A skinny woman in yellow Chinos placed her order. Music was playing in the background, beneath a hubbub of voices. It was my favourite track from one of my favourite bands.

There were three flatscreen terminals in the corner, with people hunched over two of them. I asked at the bar about the third, and paid the fee for half an hour's use.

I sat on a rocky wooden stool and tapped at the keyboard. There were clean patches on the tops of the letter keys, where thousands of fingers had rubbed off the accumulated grime of cooking and the city. Someone had left a sheet of paper beside the screen, covered in calculations and broken English. Someone else had jotted a phone number in marker pen on to the bottom corner of the screen itself.

It was the work of only minutes to discover that the nearest media office was less than half a kilometre away. The radio station VoiceTalk Digital had its studio in a converted factory building off Lisson Grove. I'd listened to VoiceTalk a few times in the past; it was mostly inane chatter about soaps and whatever was outraging the tabloids that day, but it also had a respected reviews show and it covered major news stories. It was perfect.

I hurried back out into the street, the route to the place fixed in my mind. It was close to twenty to eleven when I arrived. The station's logo was on an illuminated rectangular sign above the entrance. Inside, beside an unmanned reception desk, was a button like a domestic doorbell marked 'Outside Office Hours, Please Ring For Assistance'.

I pressed it, and paced back and forth. I suddenly caught sight of my reflection in the glass of a framed abstract painting screwed to the wall. I looked dishevelled and drawn – I could have passed for someone twice my age. Awkwardly, I smoothed my hair.

The sound of shoes clumping down steps was followed by the appearance of an attractive woman in a chunky jumper and jeans. She was carrying a wad of loose papers, and a file just like the one I'd kept my research in at home.

"Yes, can I help you? Deliveries are during office hours only, I'm afraid."

I didn't know where to begin. "It's nothing like that," I said. "I've … come here because there's nowhere else I can go. There's … er, a news story I have information about."

She frowned. "Which one?"

"None you'll know about. This is … new.

Look, er, I have a news story that I can give you, but it's complicated, and you may not believe it at first, but I have proof."

"Why don't you come back in the morning?" she said, with a smile of encouragement. "Our news editor will be in quite early."

"It can't wait," I said, more sharply than I meant to. "I'm sorry, it really can't. This is a very big deal, believe me. I promise you, you'll have a world exclusive, the biggest crime story in decades, but it can't wait, not even till tomorrow."

Her eyes narrowed a little. "Crime? Are you in trouble? Are you involved in—?"

"No, no, I promise you, it's not like that. I have proof of crimes, but there's a great danger that I'll be silenced, that it'll all be hushed up, because it's been hushed up for years. I need to talk to someone right now."

"Then tell the police."

"I can't. The criminals have friends in the police, although many of those friends might not know the whole truth. I can't risk it."

She paused, looking past me through the glass entrance. "Is anyone else going to turn up here?

278

Is this going to be a security issue?"

"No." I shook my head. "Well, I can't guarantee it, but there's nobody following me at the moment, I'm almost sure."

"Who are you, exactly? And how old are you? Where have you come from?"

"My name is Sam Hunter. I'm seventeen. I live in Hadlington."

"Hadlington?" she said, raising her eyebrows. "Why come here?"

"Because I can trust you, can't I?" I shrugged.

I could see she was wavering. She glanced at her watch.

"Follow me up," she said. "But I'm warning you, if this is some sort of gag, you are in big trouble."

She led me up two flights of stairs, into a heavily carpeted area with sofas on one side and two enormous glass panels on the other, each looking into a small studio. In one of them, an unshaven man in a *Doctor Strange* T-shirt was at a sound desk, talking into a microphone. The station's output came from a speaker on a coffee table.

"…broadcasting around the UK on DAB, and on the world wide web, this is VoiceTalk Digital, the home of debate, discussion, and chat…"

"Wait here a minute, have a seat. I'm Sarah, by the way."

"Thanks," I said weakly.

She was only gone for a matter of seconds. When she came back, she had a notepad and pen.

"As luck would have it, I have a little time," she said. "We can talk in the Meeting Room. Do you want a cup of tea or anything?"

"No, thank you," I said.

"Mind if I do?"

"No, of course not."

She showed me into a narrow room overlooking the road. The only things in it were a polished oval table and six chrome-framed chairs arranged round it. I sat down while she fetched a Styrofoam cup of milky coffee. She sat opposite me and flipped open her notepad.

"OK, Sam, tell me all about it. What are we talking here, robbery? Fraud?"

"Murder," I said.

Her expression changed. "Whoa, this is for the police. I know what you said, but this station can't start being—"

"Please, I'm begging you," I cried. "Just hear me out. Then do what you like, call who you like, but please listen to me. I have to tell someone like you, I can't trust anyone else."

She rubbed a hand across her forehead and took a sip of her coffee. "I'm probably being stupid saying this, but go on."

I told her everything, from the beginning. It all flooded out of me. She listened, taking notes and staring at me with a growing look of horror on her face. I pulled the little notebook from my jeans, straightened it out a bit and handed it to her. She turned the pages with the edge of two fingers, as if the thing would suddenly bite her. The colour drained from her cheeks.

"This notebook is … how old?" she said.

"Entries are dated 1971," I said. "And if you look in the back you'll see a printed advert for 1972 diaries."

She placed it delicately on the table. She was silent for a while.

"OK," she said at last. "First, the police really have got to know about this, and right now. But! Also, we have to get you, and this notebook, some

281

sort of reliable protection. If these Greenhills are intent on getting to you, then we have to make sure that you're so far out of their reach you might as well be on Mars. OK?"

"OK," I nodded.

"We can't broadcast anything, I'm sure you can understand that. We'd be breaking laws ourselves. Once the police are involved, it's a different matter."

"Right." I was nodding as if to make my head drop off.

"Also," she said, "your parents may be in danger, if your suspicions are right and the Greenhills might use them to frame you for something. I've got a few contacts who'll know who to call on that score, security people."

"Right, thank you."

Sarah leaned towards me. She spoke slowly and quietly. "Sam, you've been extremely brave. This is going to be over soon. You're not alone. And there was nothing you could have done to help your friends. You can't beat yourself up about that. OK?"

My vision glazed and swam. "Thanks," I muttered.
"OK?"

I nodded again. I sniffed and swiped at my nose

with the back of my hand.

There was something yellow on my knuckles. A thin line of yellow. Like my parents, like the neighbours.

I raised my hand, my mind shattering in fright, telling myself it couldn't be true.

I looked up at Sarah.

"OK? … OK? … OK? … OK?"

It wasn't my vision that swam. It was the room.

I leaped to my feet and ran, but I didn't move. I screamed out, but didn't make a sound. I kicked and raged, but stayed exactly where I was.

Sarah's features began to sag, to wrinkle, to age and shrink before my eyes. Her skin turned brittle. It split, like a map of rivers over her face. Her flesh peeled away. A skeleton sat opposite me.

The walls slid and folded, the floor beneath me opened up. Everything melted into other shapes, growing cold and dark.

I was on the bench again. The broken wooden bench outside the chip shop on the Elton Gardens estate. I was sprawled, one hand gripping the bench tightly and the other held out as if to steady myself.

"Bloody teenagers, getting pissed up." A old woman shuffled by, eating chips from a folded-back paper package in her hand.

The clock inside the chip shop said quarter past nine. Only three or four minutes since I'd last looked.

They'd got me. "You belong to us, Sam Hunter," Emma had shouted. They'd dosed me up. The journey to London, London itself, the radio station, telling my story, striking a blow against the Greenhills, all of it gone. All in my head. Three or four minutes.

No wonder they hadn't chased me when I escaped from the basement. This was their plan. Nothing elaborate, none of the dramatic fates I'd feared. It was simply a case of sending me mad. Making me one of their patients. Keeping me locked up in my own brain.

I couldn't hold it back any longer. I howled, my head in my hands, tears dripping through my fingers.

Sarah had been wrong.

I *was* alone.

Chapter Sixteen

I would not give in.

I would not submit.

I wiped my eyes dry with the sleeves of my coat, cursing my own weakness. Tears wouldn't solve anything. I had to work out a new plan.

People came and went around me. The cold seeped into my face and fingers.

I dabbed at my nose. The yellowish stuff was barely there at all now.

Whatever they'd dosed me with, it wasn't the same thing Emma had slipped me at the Halloween Ball. Until whatever drug it was wore off, the entire hallucination had seemed completely real, a world that was indistinguishable from fact.

It wasn't the same stuff they dosed my parents and the neighbours with either. Mum and Dad weren't seeing and hearing things, they weren't living in a different world, they were simply pacified and unquestioning. Besides, I'd already reasoned that the 'medication' used for them was something that needed to build up in their systems over time.

Whatever hallucinating state I'd been put into, it had cut in and cut out, quickly and completely. The effects had lasted only minutes, even though I thought several hours had gone by.

If the Greenhills were going to get me out of the way like this, by removing my ability to know truth from fiction, by keeping my mind looping around inside itself, they'd have to *keep* dosing me. Wouldn't they?

Unless what I'd experienced was the after-effects of the tranquillizer they'd shot me with in the hallway? No, that didn't seem likely. Why would after-effects suddenly start and stop like that, hours after I'd been shot?

They must have given me something while I was unconscious. Was that why Liam had still been out cold? Was that why Jo had been looking around wildly like that? Had she been in some sort of hallucinating state back there?

So why hadn't I been like that, too? Why not in the basement? Had I been shot with another dart, just minutes ago? Had someone sneaked up on me and jabbed me with a needle? That didn't seem very likely either.

Unless the Greenhills had created a drug that sat around in your system and then suddenly took hold, I couldn't see how...

I remembered something I'd read ... or had I seen it in a TV documentary? About medical devices designed to deliver regular doses of medicine automatically. Small implants, embedded under the skin. What were they called? 'Bioactive' or something like that. They were surgically implanted into patients with chronic diseases, so that they could get exact amounts of medicines without having to be in hospital all the time. These devices looked a bit like big headache pills.

With a growing sensation of dread, I reached inside my coat and under my shirt. I ran my hand around my chest. I couldn't feel anything odd. I squeezed along my arms through my sleeves. Nothing. It was only when I reached up to the back of my left shoulder that I found it.

There was a small, flattened lump. I could only feel it inside when I firmly pressed against it with my fingers. With a shaky forefinger, I traced its shape. It was an oval about the size of one of those plastic cases SD memory cards come in, a plateau that rose about a millimetre above the surface of the surrounding flesh.

I sat still, with absolutely no idea what to do.

They must have done this to other victims. To keep them confused and quiet while they were imprisoned alive in the basement. They must have done the same to Jo, and her first dose had already been delivered by the time I regained consciousness in the basement. Mine hadn't happened until more than half an hour later, when I'd escaped and was here outside the chip shop. Why? These devices must be set going at the time of implantation, so perhaps hers had been implanted half an hour before mine?

I'd been given one dose. That meant another could happen at any moment.

What was the time delay between doses? Days, hours, minutes? Was it random? Was that all part of the Greenhills' trickery, making sure I'd never know if I was in the real world or not?

I had to get that thing out of me.

I jumped to my feet but I had no clue what to do. I was standing outside the shops, in the middle of Elton Gardens – how the hell was I going to have a surgical implant taken out of my shoulder?

The hospital was on the other side of town. It would take me at least an hour to get there, even if I ran. It'd be quicker in a taxi. I could return to the station.

Correction. I could go to the station for the first time tonight.

My blood ran cold. Even if I got to the hospital, how would I know that what happened to me there would be real? I might snap out of it three hours later, and find myself right back here, all over again.

I shut my eyes. That last dose had worn off only a matter of minutes ago. How probable was it that a second had already been released into my system? Not very, at a guess. The implant would quickly run out of its drug supply if the doses were that close together, wouldn't it? I could be *reasonably* sure that my current surroundings, at this precise moment, were still real. The question was: how long would that remain true?

I had to get this bloody thing out of me *right now*!

I ran off along the main road. This was the route that all the Elton Gardens kids took to school, one that led to the giant roundabout by the supermarket. Cars flashed past, headlights glaring.

I dashed through the roundabout's echoing underpass, its stark lighting encased in squat metal cages, its floor stained with chewing gum and puddled with urine and leaks from the roof. I raced up the slope to the car park outside the supermarket, past a scattering of late-night shoppers wheeling fully laden trolleys and unloading them into hatchbacks. As I marched hurriedly into the shop, the fat security guard in the entrance lobby eyed me warily. The bright interior made me blink for a few moments. Skirting round the fruit and veg, I looked up and down for the right aisle.

I found a wide display of pots, pans and utensils, next to shelves filled with food mixers and microwave ovens. I looked back and forth, back and forth, my mind apparently incapable of concentrating on the task at hand. After what felt like days, I spotted a row of kitchen knives dangling from extended hooks, each knife sealed into a rectangular plastic package.

I picked out one with a short blade and a point at the end. Slipping it off the hook, I marched back to the checkouts. I placed the plastic package beside the woman at the scanner, while I rooted for money. All the cash I'd taken from home was still there.

"Do you have ID?" sighed the woman.

"Sorry?" I snapped.

"ID, luv. For the knife. Are you sixteen or over?"

"Yes," I said irritably.

She stared at me then and bleeped the package across the glass.

Clutching the package and receipt, I headed straight for the toilets close to the coffee shop. The heavy door swung shut behind me with a bump.

The washroom was empty. There was a row of six cubicles to the left, and hand basins to the right. The room was bathed in a sickly fluorescent light that somehow managed to be both too bright and too dim at the same time.

My hands shaking, and my breath coming in heaving gasps, I went over to the furthest basin. My reflection in the mirror looked awful. Hollow-eyed and thin-lipped, like an empty shell of skin, like someone near death putting on a brave face.

I sniffed hard and swallowed.

My fingers scratched at the knife's packaging. How were you supposed to get into this bloody thing? I tried to tear it, but couldn't. I bit at it, but it only hurt my teeth.

For Christ's sake!

I snapped. I bashed the damn thing against the basin, over and over and over and over. Tears welled in my eyes. My mouth twisted into a grimace of anger.

The door swung back and a supermarket employee sauntered in. He saw me, turned on his heels with his eyes widening and left again.

I flung the package into the basin. It slid and spun around against the smooth white porcelain. I gripped the edge of the basin, my head hanging down, sobs wracking my whole body.

Stop it! Stop being a bloody weakling and do what you came here to do!

The packaging had split in a couple of places. I forced the sharp edges apart until I could finally pull the knife free and hurled the remains of the plastic across the room.

The knife felt cold in my hand. I stared at it for a

moment, my hands trembling.

How sharp is it? I wondered.

I gently pulled the edge of the blade across the pad of my thumb. Blood welled up before I even felt the sting of the cut.

Sharp enough.

Trying to steady my breathing, I took off my coat and balled it up to one side of the basin. Then I unbuttoned my shirt and removed my arms from it, letting it flop down around my waist.

Holding my teeth together tightly, I twisted round so that I could see the back of my left shoulder in the mirror. The flattened lump looked smaller than it had felt. There was a bruise and a red mark at one end of it, where it had been inserted under my skin.

I dabbed at it with quivering fingers. There was almost no sensation of it inside my shoulder at all. If I hadn't been looking for it, I might never have even realized it was there.

Steadying myself against the basin with one hand, I gripped the knife in the other. I leaned a little closer to the mirror, twisting as far as I could to get a clear view of the lump.

The knife shook in my hand.

You'll never be a surgeon, huh? Not like…

An image flashed through my mind, of Emma firing the dispenser into my unconscious body.

Come on, time to take it out now.

Do it.

Do it!

I pressed the blade against my skin, at a point just below the lump. My hand wouldn't stop shaking. I had to press my waist against the edge of the basin instead, and use my other hand to steady the one holding the knife.

Do it!

In one unsteady movement, I ran the point in a line underneath the lump. Pain suddenly crackled through me. For a moment, blood neatly defined the incision I'd made, then spread and ran in a broad trickle down my back. Bright, red, glistening.

Shit shit shit, why hadn't I thought this through?

Leaving the knife beside the basin taps, I knocked open one of the cubicles and unspooled a thick wad of toilet paper. By the time I got back to the mirror, blood was soaking into the shirt round my waist.

I pressed the paper to the cut, but it stung so badly I had to remove it at once. For a second I stood there not knowing whether to just fling it aside or not. In the end, I stuffed the paper into my waistband, where the blood was meeting my shirt, so that at least some of it would be soaked up.

I resumed my position in front of the mirror, and raised the knife again. If I cut under and to one side, would that be enough? Could I squeeze the thing out then? I'd have to make sure I pressed in exactly the right spot, or the dispenser would only be pushed deeper in. Should I cut all around, then?

The cut felt like a dozen wasps attacking me and the angle I was twisted at to see in the mirror sent drips of red splatting into the basin.

I pressed the skin above the cut, to see if the dispenser would move. A sharp jolt of pain made me stop, and a fresh welling of blood rushed out.

Oh shit. Shit shit shit.

Using both hands to steady it, I pressed the blade to one end of the cut, at ninety degrees to the first incision. Breathing as steadily as possible, I drew it across my skin. Up, across, down, three more cuts.

The pain hacked through my mind, screaming at me to stop. The horror of what I was doing kept hammering at me. Blood. Flesh. Running, spreading, leaking out. Cutting human tissue, like a slab of meat, like *they* do!

I could hardly see the cuts, they were so smeared with blood. The knife, my fingers, the white basin – everything was covered.

I'd sliced a small, misshapen rectangle of skin. Trying to ignore the pain, I prodded at it with the point of the knife. The rectangle was gently pushed outward by the presence of the dispenser beneath. As I nudged at it, blood still oozing, it felt detached.

I cut at the edge. A little section of skin folded back. I shivered and trembled.

There was a glint of silver, in amongst the blood. My hands shaking, I turned the knife round, and pressed with the handle at the other end of the cuts.

The pain made me wince and catch my breath, but the silver moved. It definitely moved. I pressed slightly harder, moving the handle along.

Suddenly, the dispenser slipped free. I felt a weird sensation in my shoulder as it came loose.

It almost slid out, but rapidly coagulating blood kept it stuck to me. Carefully, I reached up and plucked it away, between thumb and forefinger.

With my other hand, I pulled out the wad of toilet

paper. It was heavy and red. I dropped it to the floor with a loud splat.

I held the dispenser up close to my face. It was flat and oval, as I'd thought. It seemed to be mostly a plain, dull metal, but on the lower surface was a circle of plastic, covering a tiny microchip.

I started to wipe the blood off it. The pain in my shoulder seemed almost irrelevant now, throbbing and writhing angrily, as if it knew I'd beaten it. I rubbed my thumb against the dispenser to get rid of the blood, but all I was doing was smearing it about.

My fingers were slippery. The dispenser popped out of my grasp. My heart stopped as I watched it spin and tumble.

It bounced against the washbasin with a loud ting. My hands reached out for it, but missed. It clattered around the bowl. *No, no, no, don't lose it! Don't let it drop down the drain!*

Frantically, I jammed one hand over the plughole, and let the dispenser eventually bounce to a stop against it. I scooped it up and held it tightly in my palm.

I tucked it away safely. The notebook was in one pocket of my jeans, the dispenser was in the other along with the cash from home. I had twice the evidence now. There'd be a quantity of whatever-drug-it-was left in the dispenser, enough to analyze.

I looked into the mirror. This was reality. I could be sure of that now.

There was a creaking sound.

"Don't move!"

Chapter Seventeen

"You stay right where you are."

Slowly, I turned my head. A police officer was standing with one hand holding the door ajar, the other held out towards me, fingers wide.

"S'OK," he said. "Take it easy." He unhooked the radio from his lapel and spoke into it. "I've got him, male toilets, adjacent to coffee shop."

He never took his eyes off me. I barely moved a muscle.

"S'OK, mate," he said. "You get your shirt and your coat back on, eh? Leave the knife right there by the sink. Come with me, and we'll get those nasty cuts seen to, right?"

I could tell one thing: he was scared of me.

That single thought set alarm bells ringing in my head. This guy was in his forties or fifties, he must have seen it all a hundred times before, and yet he was reacting to me – a pale, shivering, apparently self-harming teenager – as if I was a dangerous villain who might pull out a shotgun and blast him apart at any moment.

Who did he think I was? What did he think I'd done?

"C'mon, mate, you come with me. Leave the knife; that's it. Have you got anything else with you? Any other weapons?"

"No," I said.

He nodded. "Put your shirt on, yes?"

As I pulled my arms back into the sleeves, wincing as my shoulder moved, he reached over and took my rolled-up coat. He felt inside it and around the lining, keeping his gaze firmly on me. Once he was satisfied that there was nothing concealed in the coat, he handed it to me and I put it on.

"You follow me now, OK? Nobody's going to hurt you."

There was only one way in or out of the washroom. There were no windows. It was pointless to try fighting him or dodging past him – he was twice my size and ready for trouble. I tried to remember if police officers carried pepper sprays.

I took a few steps towards him. He took hold of

my arm and led me out into the supermarket. "OK, nothing to worry about. Off we go."

I expected to see a line of horrified faces, late-night shoppers all gawping at the stab-vested cop boldly arresting the scraggy teen lowlife. But apart from one or two gawping but keeping their distance, everything was pretty much as normal. The scraggy teen lowlife situation was being handled very quietly.

The alarm bells in my head were getting louder. Where had the shop's security guard gone? Wouldn't someone being arrested be a bright spot in an otherwise dull shift?

"Am I being arrested?" I said. Not that I knew much about police work, but weren't they supposed to go through the 'arresting you on suspicion of…' stuff? The cop didn't answer me. His grip on my arm tightened a little, and his pace quickened.

"Am I being arrested here?" I repeated. "Who called you?"

"Don't you worry, son, we'll get that nasty wound seen to, eh?"

My heart was racing. He's just a cop rounding up a stray, right? That supermarket employee – he called the police and told them there was a loony in the toilets, right? A routine thing. No arrests, no bother, just take the kid away, have a word, send him home, inform his parents. Right?

I wasn't dreaming. I wasn't drugged. This was the real world, I knew that for certain. The dispenser was safely tucked into my pocket, it wouldn't be fooling me any more.

A cold sensation of dread grew inside me. I was tired and dazed.

"It's *them*, isn't it?" I muttered. I almost felt like laughing, cackling like a maniac. "They knew I'd turn up somewhere. And they sent you to get me. What did they tell you? Am I an escaped psychiatric patient, is that it? I bet that's it."

This was reality, but I'd forgotten: reality was whatever the Greenhills said it was. Truth was whatever they told people.

I actually began to giggle.

The cop was getting irritated. He squeezed my arm tightly. We'd reached the supermarket's entrance lobby now. A wall of freezing-cold air washed around me.

Outside, it had started to rain. Big, slow drops, quickly filling all the dips in the car park. Street lights glittered on wet surfaces. A guy in a high-visibility jacket pushed a long train of empty, clanking trolleys.

The cop marched me over to a police car parked some distance away, close to the road and the slope that dipped down to the underpass. There was a hefty, unmarked BMW next to it. As we approached, a second officer got out of the patrol car and a figure in a tan raincoat got out of the BMW. As I got closer, I saw that it was Leonard Greenhill.

Two cops, and the *chief constable*. What's wrong with this picture? I giggled again. Hysteria.

"Are we going to the hospital?" I said.

None of them spoke. The second cop was carrying something that looked like handcuffs. He was burly and saturnine, much younger than the first one. As the headlights of traffic on the roundabout swung past, I caught glimpses of two more figures in the back of the BMW. A man and a woman, I thought.

The rain was starting to intensify. The second cop rolled up to me.

"Pull up the right leg of your jeans, please, sir."

"Sorry?"

"Pull up the right leg of your jeans, please, sir."

It wasn't handcuffs he was carrying, it was an

electronic tag. For a moment or two, I struggled and kicked, but I quickly realized there was no way I'd avoid it. He crouched down and clicked the thick grey loop round my ankle.

As soon as the tag was on, the first cop led me to the police car. Leonard Greenhill watched me impassively. I wanted to stare back at him, my face filled with defiance and anger, but somehow I couldn't meet his gaze. I was exhausted and defeated. The pain in my shoulder throbbed and screeched.

The first cop ushered me on to the back seat, cradling the top of my head as I got in. He slapped the door shut beside me. The police car was warm, quiet and roomy. A couple of red LEDs flicked and ticked on the dashboard. Rain pattered in waves against the windscreen. There was a faint smell of pine.

I expected the two cops to get in and drive me away immediately, but they both went round to the other side of the BMW and started talking to the chief constable. All I could see of the other two figures in the BMW were vague shapes in the gloom.

I pulled up my trouser leg. The tag felt loose but heavy, obviously made to withstand a lot of misuse. There was a slightly thicker section to one side of it, where a tiny green light shone.

There was no escape now. They could track me wherever I went.

No way out. I struggled to stop my heart sinking into an abyss.

Maybe, if the two cops were going to drive me away, I could explain things to them on the way. I could show them my evidence. I might be able to persuade them to protect me, instead of throwing me to the Greenhills? They'd believe that their boss was part of a family of homicidal maniacs, wouldn't they? Wouldn't they?

I half laughed, half sobbed. Yeah. Of course they would. I was an escaped psychiatric patient, remember? It's not like I'd be paranoid, or make anything up now, would I?

The cops and Leonard Greenhill were still talking. What *about*, for God's sake?

Anger began to swell up through me.

I still had the evidence. Enough to expose the truth. I still had to get it to someone I could trust, to tell the world in a way that couldn't be discredited, or ignored, or deleted.

That much hadn't changed.

The change was the tag round my ankle. What I no longer had was time. I was minutes from having the evidence taken away from me forever. As soon as we got to a police station, or even a hospital, I'd be searched.

They could track me, they could find me anywhere. My only hope was to outrun them.

They'd made my capture low-key. The absolute minimum fuss needed to make it look authentic, official.

I could use that against them.

They were out there, and I was in here alone. The cars were parked barely ten metres from the slope that went down into the underpass. The rain was getting heavier, and therefore noisier. It was dark. If I could get out of the police car without being seen, then I could surely make it to the far side of the roundabout. They might not even bother chasing me straight away, not now they had me tagged. They might think they had time to scoop me up whenever they liked. They didn't even know I had the notebook, and nobody had seen me keep the drug dispenser.

It was all a question of finding a safe home for my

evidence. There'd be no point hiding it, burying it or something, because when they caught me it'd be lost for good. But, with whatever head start I could get on them…

If I could get to someone I could entrust my evidence to… If I could just get to a phone…

I might only have minutes, I thought. *But minutes were better than nothing.*

This would be my last chance.

If I didn't take it, everything would count for nothing and the Greenhills would carry on, hiding in their house of blood forever. Once they caught me, I'd be dead. There was no doubt whatsoever.

All this flashed through my mind in a split second.

I clicked open the police car door beside me. The sound of the rain suddenly increased, and drips spattered along my side.

The cops were facing away from me blocking Leonard Greenhill's view of the police car.

Keeping low, I slipped out into the rain, opening the door only enough to allow me to squeeze through. I shut the door gently. They'd have to look inside now to see I was gone.

Crouching, I turned and ran for the underpass, my

heart pounding. I expected to hear shouts behind me at any moment, but none came. As I reached the slope, I threw myself down, out of sight, and looked back.

The ice-cold rain was dropping in sheets now. Already, I was almost soaked. Despite the street lights, and the bright rectangle of the supermarket, the police car and the BMW were barely visible behind the downpour. If I could hardly see them, they wouldn't be able to see me either.

Without hesitating, I pelted down the slope and through the underpass. My footsteps echoed against the concrete walls. I paused at the far end and glanced back, then I ran out into the rain again, back along the road into Elton Gardens.

Headlights kept rearing up behind me. Every time, my heart skipped a beat, anticipating flashing blue lights and the whoop of a siren. I didn't dare look over my shoulder. I could feel the tag on my ankle with every step. Rain ran through my hair and down my face.

Soon, I was back at the line of shops. The off-licence was closed now, and the lights in the chippie were being switched off.

Possible plans of action were cascading through my mind. I still had the money. A bus or a train might not be a good idea; I'd be effectively trapped – they could simply wait for me at the other end. Unless I got off at some random point. And go where?

No, a taxi would be better. More flexible, more routes to follow, fast and unpredictable. I could head into London, exactly as I'd planned before. I could get to the real VoiceTalk, or something similar. The taxi driver might know something nearer.

Would I have time? Would Leonard Greenhill risk involving more police, who'd cut off whatever route I took?

I ran for the station. Some of the street lights were out and in my panic, in the rain and the darkness, I soon realized I'd taken a wrong turn somewhere. Now they knew where I was, but I didn't! Fighting back a tide of despair, I stopped to get my bearings.

I was on a short, narrow road, bordered on one side by bungalows with ugly concrete fascias, and on the other side by the plain brick walls of houses in the neighbouring street. There was a faded wooden 'No Ball Games' sign screwed to a wall. One of the two working lamp posts had a bedraggled photocopy stuck to it, showing a picture of a dog beneath the words, 'Missing – please help' handwritten in thick marker pen.

I spun on my heels. Which way? I turned and went back the way I'd come. I'd see somewhere I recognized soon, I thought. I had to keep my head down, to keep the rain out of my eyes. I almost ran into her.

Emma.

I let out a cry of fright. She was less than three metres from me. For long seconds, I was frozen.

She smiled at me. A broad, reptilian grin of delight. Her eyes were wide, alight, shocking. Her face was wet with rain, her hair tied back.

"I told you to be a good boy."

She reached into her raincoat. She took out a medical scalpel, and held it delicately in her long fingers.

Chapter Eighteen

Panic took over. I almost fell over, my legs all but buckled beneath me. I ran along the street, then stopped and turned. She was walking towards me, in no hurry at all.

I stumbled over to the nearest of the bungalows. A light was on, behind curtains. I jabbed at the bell, heard it chime.

She was closer.

"Hello!" I yelled. "Help! Help me!"

I banged on the door and hit the bell again.

I waited only a second or two more. Nobody was answering. I scrambled around a pair of wheelie bins and went next door. More lights inside. I pounded the door with my fist.

"Hello! Help me! Please open up! Please!"

The lights went out. I tottered backwards.

She was closer.

I ran on down the street, the rain lashing and

hissing. More lights in a bungalow further on. Someone had to answer. Someone had to listen. This time, I pulled at the letterbox.

"Hello? Is anyone there? This is an emergency! Please come to the door!"

I waited. I didn't dare look behind me.

"Open up!" I yelled. I slapped at the door's frosted glass. "Listen to me! I'm begging you! Open the door!"

A light came on right behind the door. A shape appeared in the hallway beyond, rippled by the glass.

"Piss off, you bloody drunk!"

The light switched off again.

Emma was ten metres away.

"Fire! Fiiiiiire!" The words burned my throat. They were lost, in the roar of the rain, washed away.

Emma was five metres away.

I ran on blindly into the darkness beyond the yellowish glow of the last street light. Down a narrow alleyway, with tall wooden fences to either side, emerging into another street.

I can outrun her. Lose her. That's what I can do, I thought.

In my panic, the tag on my ankle was almost forgotten. I wasn't thinking straight. She knew exactly where I was. There was no escape.

At the end of this second street, I suddenly knew where I was. This was close to the point at which Elton Gardens bordered the park.

In moments, I was standing on the long path that edged the park's huge, open lawns. Light from the lamp posts along the path was filled with vertical lines of rain. The sky was low and pitch-black, and it was difficult to make out anything further than twenty metres past the glow of the lamps.

Off somewhere to the left, the river, the green footbridge and the path up to Maybrick Road. I wouldn't go that way, too much chance of running into the rest of the Greenhills. Too close to home.

I dashed off across the lawns, plunging into the shadows, my feet squelching on the sodden grass. Unable to see much, I toppled over twice, sprawling forward painfully, palms thrust out and sliding along the mud. I staggered to my feet, suddenly conscious of how soaked to the skin I was, how cold and out of breath.

Dragging myself on, I reached a tightly packed group of trees that clustered close to the children's swings and climbing frames. Leaning against a trunk, in the shelter of the overhead branches, I shook some of the water off myself and took a few deep breaths. My eyes were getting accustomed to the dark. I could see outlines of more trees in the distance, and the faint, rain-scattered glow of the town. I could just about make out the brow of the hill on Maybrick Road. Below that snaked the river, which would now be slowly swelling with the pouring rain.

Suddenly, there was a flash of movement beside me!

With a low, blood-chilling cry, Emma kicked out and knocked me flying. I tumbled on to my back. She was on top of me before I knew what was happening.

We grappled fiercely. I was stronger than her, but with the scalpel gripped tightly in her hand, it was all I could do to stop her slashing me across the face. Her expression was gleeful and alive with spiteful pleasure.

With a heave, I managed to push her to one side. I scrambled to find my feet before she could lunge at me again.

"Like the tracker?" she cried. "Another of my ideas. Good, isn't it?" She dangled her smartphone at me. "Pinpoints you to within two metres. C'mon, boy, let's race for your life."

Her delight at taunting me only made me angry. With a yell of fury, I flew at her, grasping for the smartphone. She snatched it out of my reach and, with my attention on the phone, swung the blade of the scalpel at my chest.

There was a burst of pain, and a dark patch began to spread on the front of my shirt. I leaped aside, crying out like the wounded prey I'd become.

Emma almost skipped with enjoyment. She was getting ready to pounce again.

Mindlessly, I turned and fled. Outside the shelter of the trees, the rain began to pummel me once more. The thud of my footsteps turned sharper as I left the grass and crossed the tarmac of the play area. I skirted the swings and the slide, running in any direction that would take me away...

But I'd never shake her off. I was prey now.

My only choice was to kill her before she killed me. It was me or her, wasn't it?

I slowed down. By now, I was close to the river. The high-pitched slamming of the rain was mingling with the low gurgle of the sluggish waters. I stood on the foot-worn track that followed the curve of the river bank.

I was out in the open, the river behind me. There was no way she could approach me unseen.

I waited, feeling icy rainfall trickle at my neck. My heartbeat thumped in my ears.

She was only a vague outline at first. Walking steadily, her hips swaying.

She'd put the scalpel away. She held something that looked like a small cleaver, or an axe. With a shudder, I recognized it from the display of operating tools in the basement's glass cabinets.

I stood my ground. Her pace quickened.

I shook with nerves, with cold, with terror. Her pace quickened again.

Without a sound, she raised the cleaver to one side and ran at me. As she bore down, I grabbed at her arms and her momentum threw us over.

Emma was back on her feet before me. She aimed a hard kick at my side as I scrambled on all fours, and I rolled over in agony. Suddenly catching a dull reflection on metal, I flinched to one side and the cleaver buried itself in the grass beside my head.

I hooked my foot round her leg and pulled sharply. She toppled back, but again she was quicker than me. As I raced towards her, she punched me square across the jaw. I spun, dazed.

By the time I'd regained my senses, she'd retrieved the cleaver. I jumped back, and back again, as she slashed it through the air in front of me. Her face was still a horrible mask of joy.

As she swung the blade again, I lunged. I barrelled into her, knocking her off her feet, and pinned her to the grass.

She clawed at my face. I tried to ignore the pain, but it distracted me long enough to allow her to thud her knee into my stomach. Winded, I almost let her go, but managed to keep a grip on the lapels of her raincoat. She twisted, pulling us both over. We rolled, struggling to strike at each other, the rain lashing into her face, then mine.

She pulled a hand free, and aimed a sharp blow at the cut in my chest. The stab of pain made me scream. Stars flashed in my eyes. The next thing I knew, she was astride me, raising the cleaver in one hand, high above her head.

My hand shot out to grab her wrist. The cleaver shook as she wriggled to free it. I was gradually forcing her arm round, until she'd have to drop the weapon. Suddenly, she snatched the cleaver with her other hand and brought it down on top of me.

The only thing I had time to do was raise my arm in defence. The cleaver bit through the sleeve of my coat and deep into my arm. I howled.

The agony goaded me into fury. I pulled the cleaver out, a spurt of blood following it, and flung it over my head. I heard it splash into the river. Before Emma could react, I had both my hands round her throat.

I squeezed. I wanted to kill her. I *had* to kill her. For everything she'd done, everything her family had done. See how they liked it!

I felt the flesh of her throat tighten. Her face reddened, her eyes bulged. Gradually, her expression changed from glee to fear, from murderous triumph to despair.

But if I killed her, because I could, because I wanted to, I'd be like *them*.

Horrified, I flung her aside. She sprawled on the wet grass, rain beating at her back, coughing and spluttering. Furiously, she pulled out her phone, tapped at it a couple of times, and stuffed it back into her raincoat. She rubbed at her neck.

"I won't kill," I said. "I won't become one of you."

I thought about which way I should run. She was already standing up, swaying slightly.

"Weakling," she said.

She kicked me in the side of the head.

I didn't black out but my head swam wildly. Then I was aware of voices.

"Where's my antique amputation knife?" Byron Greenhill.

A pause. "He threw it in the river." Emma.

"Oh, for goodness' sake! You promised me you'd look after it."

"That can come out of your allowance, young lady." Caroline Greenhill.

"That's not fair!"

"It's perfectly fair. If you can't look after things, you must pay for them."

"Can we get out of this rain? I'll catch my death." Ken Greenhill.

I looked up, still feeling unsteady. They were in a semicircle behind me, umbrellas raised. The four of them.

Byron Greenhill stooped down. He spoke to me as if I was five years old. "Well, you've given us quite a little adventure, haven't you, hmm? Can you stand?

Can you walk?"

I didn't have the strength to answer. I crawled up on to my knees.

Byron grasped me under one arm, Caroline the other. I was frogmarched along, sometimes walking for myself, sometimes being hauled upright.

"You see, you didn't need me," grumbled Ken Greenhill. "I could have stayed warm, at home."

"Objection noted," said Byron wearily.

We crossed the green metal footbridge, the river thundering beneath our feet. We walked up the hill, and back into Priory Mews. The rain continued to belt down relentlessly. I felt water inside my boots.

My head was clearing and the reality of what they were doing suddenly scorched into my head like a burst of lava. I began to struggle. Byron and Caroline tightened their grip.

"Shall I take his feet?" said Emma.

"No, darling, we're nearly there," said Byron. "Mummy's got a syringe if he gets uppity."

We were approaching the Priory. Panic began to overtake me again.

I stared across the road, to the houses. There were people standing in the windows of all three. The

Giffords, the Daltons. My parents. They waved at me. All of them.

I screamed out. I thrashed. I became a dead weight, kicking and yelling.

"Mum!" I screamed out. "Muuuum! Dad! Don't let them take me! Don't let them take me! Please! Please! Mum!"

They waved. Goodbye, Sam. Then they were out of sight. I was dragged along the gravel driveway of the Priory, up the steps, into the house. I thrashed and howled. The front door slammed shut behind me, cutting off the night, and the rain, and the sound of my voice.

Chapter Nineteen

I've been here, in the basement, for two weeks now, I think. It's hard to tell.

I'm feeling so much better. The injections mean I don't feel any pain.

I'm inside one of the glass booths. I'm where Kat Brennan used to be. Byron and Emma brought this little desk down for me to use. It's a really nice piece of furniture.

I've filled three notebooks, writing all this down. Once I've recorded what's happened, they want me to keep notes on my forthcoming operations. There are going to be quite a lot of them. They want me to note down how I'm feeling, my impressions as my body is changed.

After the experiments are over, the notebooks I've filled will become part of the official family archive. A very important part, Byron says, because they don't have many records as detailed as mine.

The notebook I stole is back in the archive. The rain had caused some damage. Byron wasn't at all pleased. Emma was very angry with me, too, because I nearly killed her, but I think she's forgiven me now. At first she talked a great deal about revenge, and about making me suffer, but Byron pointed out to her that I, with my journalistic skills, represented an unusual opportunity, and that I should be considered a long-term subject for study. He told her she still had a lot to learn, that she hadn't made full use of Liam and Jo, which was wasteful.

Jo lived for three days. Her liver was transplanted into Gottfried Hugelgrun, who'd been in need of a new one for a while. Most of the rest of her ended up incinerated.

Liam was taken apart, too, piece by piece. Emma made three living specimens from him, using various grafting techniques and artificial organs. Part of him is still in the next room. I hear it cry out from time to time.

The disappearance of all three of us was neatly accounted for. They hadn't reported me as an escaped psychiatric patient, as I'd assumed at first. What the rest of the world believed was this: the day we claimed to be around town doing our geography project was the day I killed them both, then burned their bodies to dust. I'd been off my head on drugs. Later, filled with remorse, I stabbed myself to death using a knife, following an escape from police custody outside the supermarket. So mad, it had to be true.

The story was all Emma's idea. She's full of ideas.

The first time I escaped, when I got out of this basement, was a big surprise for the Greenhills. I showed up a loophole in their security. It's a loophole that's now been closed.

The second time I escaped, from the police car, was exactly the reverse. It had been expected. Chief Constable Leonard Greenhill had deliberately distracted his two constables, knowing that I'd have an opportunity to make a run for it. The reason? Partly to back up the story Emma had invented, but mostly to give Emma a treat. I'd caused the family a certain amount of trouble. They wanted something back. I was an evening's entertainment.

The truth will come out. One day. Someone will read these words.

I'm feeling better. The pain has been taken away, so that I can write.

I am part of Emma's apprenticeship. The last part, her final supervised project. She's already removed my stomach. A machine does that work now. It's functioning well, I'm told. Later, my shaved head is to be mapped out, ready for surgery. I'm going to have an extra brain, an external one. As I sit here at the desk, I can see a glass jar. Inside it, something pulses and grows. That will be part of me, too. I don't know what part yet.

Emma is coming towards me. Time to stop writing for the day.

Collect the whole series ...

ISBN: 978-1-84715-453-8
EISBN: 978-1-84715-504-7

Frozen Charlotte

Alex Bell

Following the sudden death of her best friend, Sophie hopes that spending the summer with family on a remote Scottish island will be just what she needs. But the old schoolhouse, with its tragic history, is anything but an escape. History is about to repeat itself. And Sophie is in terrible danger...

ISBN: 978-1-84715-455-2
EISBN: 978-1-84715-573-3

Sleepless

Lou Morgan

The pressure of exams leads Izzy and her friends to take a new study drug they find online. But one by one they succumb to hallucinations, nightmares and psychosis. The only way to survive is to stay awake...

... if you dare

Bad Bones
Graham Marks

Gabe makes a discovery that could be the answer to all his problems. But taking the Aztec gold disturbs the spirit of an evil Spanish priest hell-bent on revenge. Can Gabe escape the demon he's unleashed?

ISBN: 978-1-84715-454-5
EISBN: 978-1-84715-505-4

Dark Room
Tom Becker

When Darla and her dad move to Saffron Hills, she hopes it'll be a new start. But she stands no chance of fitting in with the image-obsessed crowd at her new school. Then one of her classmates is killed while taking a photo of herself. When more teens die it appears that a serial killer is on the loose – the 'Selfie Slayer'. Can Darla unmask the killer before it's too late?

ISBN: 978-1-84715-457-6
EISBN: 978-1-84715-645-7

Also available as ebooks

Read on for the opening chapter of *Bad Bones*...

RED EYE

Some
things
are
best
left
buried

BAD
BONES

GRAHAM MARKS

ISBN: 978-1-84715-454-5
EISBN: 978-1-84715-505-4

'Dope will get you through a time of no money better than money will get you through a time of no dope.' Gabe had read that in one of his dad's old underground, hippy comic books, he didn't remember which one. That was before his dad sold all his comics and his vinyl record collection and old-school stereo system. Before he lost his job and things started to get shitty.

That really wasn't so long ago, although it seemed like they'd been in a Time Of No Money forever. Everything had changed, and none of it for the better. Not one single damn bit.

Gabe sat on the street bench, his bike propped up next to him, watching the late-afternoon traffic go by on Ventura. Thousands of people, all with a destination, a purpose. All with money in their wallets and purses, driving on to the next stage in their sweet lives, or their neat homes, or their great jobs. None of which applied to him, his mom, dad or little sister, Remy. They were all stuck in a house he knew for a fact was worth way less than what was owed on it, and with, so far as he could see, no chance of putting that to rights.

His mother cut coupons to save money at the supermarket like it was her religion, and everything they ate was either 'no brand', or had about ten seconds left on the 'eat by' date, or both. His dad tried to keep a brave face, but didn't always succeed, and only his sister appeared not to have a care in the world. But then Remy was nine years old. Gabe remembered being that age – when the future was always a cartoon-bright tomorrow and your life was a game. He looked down at his scuffed, frayed sneakers; it was a lot harder to think like that when you were sixteen and tomorrow did not look like it was going to be promising anything any time soon.

He stood up, stretching. He could feel the tension building in his muscles, the frustration at his total inability to figure out a way in which he could solve his family's problems; even fixing *something* would be better than doing nothing.

"Maybe…" Gabe muttered to himself, grabbing his backpack, then getting on his bike, "…it'll have to be the dope."

He was about to move off when his phone

chirruped: his mom's ringtone. He let the call go to voicemail, not ready to listen to whatever it was she had to say in her often tired-to-the-bone voice; it was hardly likely to be good news. No, he was not going to go home just yet, to the wired undercurrent of resentment that there was between him and his dad nowadays.

Gabe watched for a suitable gap in the unending stream of cars and slipped neatly into place. He had nowhere to go, but at least he might shift the dark cloud that seemed to be sitting right on top of him if he rode until it hurt. And while he rode he could think about Benny's offer.

What took him off Ventura and up towards the canyon Gabe didn't know. He'd been there before, any number of times. Generally either with friends, to get a beer buzz on, or with a girlfriend, when he had a girlfriend, for some time alone. Right now, though, with the sun beginning to set, the canyon – empty, serene, somewhere completely elsewhere – felt like the perfect place to be.

He had hybrid Nutrak tyres on the bike, old now,

though still with a few more miles left in them yet. Best of both worlds, good on and off the road, the salesman had said, back when Gabe had had spare cash to splash, and the man hadn't been bullshitting. He took to the pathway, well beaten by dog walkers and hikers, and rode into this small piece of wilderness, surrounded by the endless sprawl of LA.

He knew exactly where he wanted to be, and some ten minutes later he was up on top of a huge, smooth rock, his bike left at its graffiti-covered base. Lying down, using his backpack for a pillow, he felt the warmth the rock had soaked up during the day and was now giving off as the temperature began to drop. He was tired; tired of worrying and tired of thinking too hard about how bad things were. And they had to be bad for him to even consider working for dope-dealing Benny as an option.

Gabe closed his eyes, shutting out the world, and let the quiet chatter, hum and drone of the canyon wash over him…

He didn't know what had woken him; probably it had been the chill in the air, because he was only wearing a T-shirt and jeans. The sky, dark as it ever got in LA, had no moon yet and only a scattering of stars. Gabe sat up, scrambled around in his backpack and found his phone: 7:23. He'd slept for ages, out for the count too, as there was another missed call from his mom. It was late, so she'd no doubt be worried, and he was hungry now – hungry enough not to care about the mood round the dinner table. Time to go home.

Gabe slid down the rock, now cooler to the touch, most of its heat given back to the night, and got his bike. Standing for a moment he debated what to do, finally admitting there was no way it would be a good idea to ride out. He was going to have to walk the twisting path, which clung like ivy to the steep hillsides.

As he set off, Gabe thought about calling his mom, but decided not to. She'd only ask what he was doing, who he was with and where he was. "Well, Ma, I just woke up, alone in the canyon," wasn't what she'd want to hear. He'd figure out a better story by the time he got home.

And, kind of like the way life often is, everything went fine until it didn't.

Even when you're trying hard to be careful, if nothing goes wrong for long enough you get cocky and the lazy part of your brain stops paying as much attention as it should. That was how Gabe failed to notice how unstable the pathway was. The next step he took, the ground unexpectedly gave way, he lost his balance and, arms flailing, he fell.

It wasn't all bad. The drop turned out to be not so steep or so very far down, and also he let go of his bike and it didn't come tumbling after him. Gabe, who was fit enough and good enough to be in the school athletics team, managed the fall pretty well, skidding down the side of the narrow arroyo, arms and legs held close in. He came to a stop, slightly winded, a bit bruised but with nothing broken, in a bed of dried-up mud.

There'd been a short, sharp late-summer storm, a pretty spectacular one, the previous week. The sky had turned coal-tar black in the middle of the day, there was thunder and it seemed like a ton of water per square metre had fallen in about two minutes flat. Drains had blocked, gutters overflowed, dogs went crazy, traffic snarled up and then, as quick as it had started, it was over. All that water had had to go somewhere, and in the canyon a deluge hurtled downwards, finding any exit it could; it ripped out small trees and dislodged rocks and earth from the arroyo – brick-dry from the long, hot summer – as it raced towards the San Fernando valley.

Picking himself up, Gabe found he was in a two- maybe three-metre deep, four-metre wide cut that wouldn't have been there before the storm. As he looked around for the best way to get back up to his bike, the moon peeked over the ragged treeline behind him. Its soft, monochrome light made it seem like he was standing in an old grainy photographic negative; it gave everything a weird, spooky look.

A metre or so away from him it also picked out the distinctive shape of a human skull.

Do YA Read Me?

Do YA Read Me? is a brand new platform for all things YA. From author insights to jacket reveals, book reviews to sneak peeks – we've got it covered.

Whether you're into romance or horror, dystopia or geekery, this is the place for you.

doYAreadme.tumblr.com

Follow us on Twitter @doYAreadme